THE COERCED KILLER

By

Paul Howard Surridge

The trials and tribulations of a fundamentally good man, coerced to kill

THE COERCED KILLER

© 2020

THE COERCED KILLER

CONTENTS

CHAPTER ONE - OUT OF

CONTROL

We are what we think about, and our dreams subconsciously shape our reality. Since time immemorial, man has been gifted with the power of cognition, the natural ability to acquire knowledge of the world around him, and the perception to understand that knowledge and the judgement of reason and intuition. Our waking hours are fed with visual images, sounds, and experiences that fuel our perception of life and our interactions with others. For some who have impaired empathy, no remorse, and disinhibited and egotistical traits, it can lead to murder on scale. When we kill, our sub-conscious mind takes over and we access scenes from past and future lives, both real and imagined.

If we met in the street tomorrow, I would introduce myself to you as Christopher Jason. Not my real name, but one I legally adopted after leaving prison. I served a lengthy sentence for a murder I did not commit. My birth name is Lawrence Hogarth. Before my imprisonment I had a good life compared to most. I ran a successful business in London, selling antiques, antiquarian books, and art. If asked, I would like to think friends would describe me as inquisitive, well-balanced, motivated and someone that loved life and enjoyed new challenges. Being in prison changed me in so many ways. I became withdrawn and unpredictable. I dreaded social interactions where I would be quizzed about my past. I wanted to drift into a reclusive life not having to think about everyday realities. Inherently, that was not me, and I had to fight off that malaise if I were to have a life worth living. Occasionally, I would do and say things that were totally out of character. I can be erratic in decision making sometimes doing the opposite of what is expected of me. It is said *time is a great healer* and I truly hope that is the case in the remaining years left for me.

The grey skies and constant winter drizzle drained me, and I longed for the warm, penetrating summer sun to return. Winter in England could be depressing. My instinct for pleasure and entertainment withered as the darker months took hold. Friends seemed to disappear for weeks on end without word, retreating to the warmth and security of their urban lofts.

It was Monday and the ebb and flow of lunchtime in central London was gaining its regular momentum. I was waiting to order lunch in a restaurant I often visited. The thin T-shirts and shorts that had been so evident a few weeks before, had been exchanged for warm sweaters, denim jeans, waterproof jackets, and umbrellas. People rushed past the restaurant window, eager to avoid the downpour. I could hear faint snatches of conversation. My choice of eatery was not predicated on its good food or impeccable service - quite the contrary. The food was mediocre at best and the service was questionable. I went there out of laziness; it was just a ten-minute walk from the studio. An antique, antiquarian book, and art business I had started on Kings Road, Chelsea, some years earlier. My trusted colleague and good friend, Mandy, now ran the Chelsea studio as I had since expanded into a second studio in the city, where I now spent most of my time. They were both profitable, allowing me to enjoy a reasonably good life. I was gregarious by nature; people and their lives fascinated me. I enjoyed close friendships and indulged myself in adventure travel, vintage cars, and a lovely but tiny house in Knightsbridge. Life was good and I knew it. Every year, I chose to support a charity. I would donate a percentage of my profits, and, if I had the time, I would arrange a fundraiser, often linked to my travels. I thought it morally right that people as fortunate as me should share their success.

I would always arrive at the restaurant early, at least early enough to miss the crowds. And, if I were fortunate, I would be guaranteed my preferred table at the window, where I would take up residence and daydream. Today was no different. I sat and gazed out of the window which looked onto Villiers Street, running parallel to Charing Cross Station. It was then that I saw her.

She was in her mid-thirties, stunningly attractive and elegantly dressed in a long, jet-black coat, with a rust brown fur collar that fit tightly around her neck. She held high a bright red umbrella that matched her lipstick. She stood motionless, ignoring the torrential rain and the people that scampered past. The sadness in her face told a story. Her arms were crossed as though she were standing at the graveside of a loved one, bidding a final farewell. She was unaware that I was watching her.

I was distracted by voices at a nearby table and became lost in the melee of conversation. A couple at the next table were engrossed in an intimate exchange. Their eyes, bright and piercing, sparkled. Businessmen, keen to impress their colleagues, speculated about the declining stock market, politics and wars around the world, and the growing immigrant crisis as people desperately tried to escape their homelands in search of a better life. Others were simply consumed in everyday conversation. It was a noisy and animated scene, one that clearly attracted people to dine there, but I felt strangely alone and isolated.

Again, I looked out of the window and watched people going about their business. I wondered what life was like for them, where they lived, the people they loved, their motivations and challenges. Neatly driven lines of rain quickly worked their way to the bottom of the window frame. The condensation partly obscured my view. A waiter I knew well approached the table to take my order. His attitude was surly; it irritated me. I was a regular and he had served me more times than I cared to remember. I had always tipped generously, but that seemed to count for little. Eyes closed, I could describe his face in minute detail and imitate his voice so convincingly that his own mother would be fooled. I ordered a meal and a bottle of wine rather than the usual solitary glass. Perhaps I had arrived at that defining moment when social drinking made its leap into dependency, and I would never be the same again.

The heavens opened, thunder clapped, and the rain came down in torrents. The condensation on the window thickened to choke my view. It was impossible to see people's faces in any detail. As far as I could make out, her stance and expression had changed little since I first set eyes upon her. She filled my view and everything else was obliterated. I wanted to know who she was and why she seemed so unhappy. My meal and wine arrived unceremoniously, briefly breaking the spell. I poured a large glass and hurriedly gulped a mouthful as if it were my last. I knew my curiosity for this woman was out of the ordinary. I would not have noticed her normally, but there was just something about her. The restaurant was full to bursting and the hubbub of conversation had become incoherent. I took another large gulp of wine and became engrossed in people's conversations.

My eyes returned to the window. I wiped the condensation with a serviette and looked out. She was no longer there. She had gone. An odd feeling of loss came over me. For some inexplicable reason, I felt cheated. She had stepped out of my life without warning. It felt as though my soulmate had said goodbye for a final time. My eyes scanned the street through the blurred window to no avail. I got up from the table, stumbled desperately to the door, and opened it. I stepped onto the street, my head turning this way and that, hoping to catch sight of her.

A cold chill ran straight through me. The warmth of the restaurant was quickly replaced by the hard reality of winter on the street. The rain intensified and within seconds, I was soaked. I had left my jacket and overcoat inside. People hurried past and stared at me amidst my desperate bid to catch sight of her. Their attention was of little consequence. I had to find her. The absurdity of the situation escaped me as I bobbed and weaved among the crowd. I did not give a second thought to the meal that sat patiently waiting for me at the table, nor my jacket, overcoat, and briefcase that remained slung across the back of my chair.

Finally, I stopped to catch my breath. I was sure I saw her crossing the road. Barely able to contain my excitement, I ran at full speed into the street and was confronted by a truck that was almost upon me. I found the pavement just in time, but she had vanished. The entrance to Piccadilly Circus underground station was in front of me. I had no time to speculate, so I blindly assumed this was her most likely direction. My hunch proved correct. She was there, about to travel down an escalator. I followed but was hindered by an army of people going in the same direction. Like a column of ants, they marched in double quick time, eager to navigate their journeys. Frustrated, I watched her sail through the barrier toward the Northern Line. I forced my way through the crowds as best I could but on reaching the barrier, my journey ended abruptly. Of course, I did not have a ticket! I stared into the distance. My foolish antics had created chaos as passenger numbers rapidly increased behind me causing a bottleneck. I knew it would be impossible to find her now.

There was no time to get a ticket, and if there were, which direction would I take? She was gone.

Undeterred by the chaos, I stood at the barrier, at a loss for what to do. Eventually, I came to my senses. Security staff approached. Not relishing the prospect of being frog marched out of the station, I turned and decided a final burst of energy would take me to the escalator and the exit. I ducked low among the crowd and pushed hard against the flow, creating a space for my retreat. I was already likely considered a madman, so anything I did now would not be considered out of character.

My tactic worked. People desperately tried to avoid me, but the sheer volume of individuals meant progress was slow. The harder I pushed, and the more erratic my actions, the further I went. The momentum grew and my path became more visible. The escalator that I had sailed down earlier was just ahead. This time, I would be going in the opposite direction and would need to run up as fast as I could, moving against the human tide. I glanced back as I sprinted, expecting to be pursued. As I reached the top of the escalator, I was breathing heavily. I walked quickly toward the exit the ordeal had taken its toll. There were only a few people going in my direction now, but the crowds kept coming toward me in droves. I could see daylight ahead.

In contrast to the scores of people around me who were sensibly dressed to ward off an arctic frost, I was remarkably conspicuous in just my shirt and trousers. Once more, I found myself bracing against the elements. As I made my way back to the restaurant, I began to question my sanity. What on earth was I doing? Why had I left the restaurant, deserting my possessions on the back of a chair to undertake a manic, half-clothed chase through the streets of London in search of a woman I did not know? This hardly represented a normal state of mind. As the adrenaline wore off, I began to shiver. I was soaked through and my body was aching. Over and over, I chastised myself. Why had I followed her? What had I expected to achieve? People were staring again. I knew what they were thinking. It was the same question I had asked myself. "What fool goes out on the streets of London half clothed on a cold, wet winter's day?" I returned to the restaurant and entered. It was full to bursting. The warmth was immediate, and the noise was deafening as alcohol-laden people raised their voices to compete with the din around them. Wet and cold to the touch, I was subjected to a raft of sniggers and indignant comments as I forced my way back to my chair and slumped down. I was exhausted. The remainder of the lukewarm wine in my glass disappeared in an instant. The rest of the bottle was consumed in a similar fashion. I took up my look-out post once more and drifted.

CHAPTER TWO -

DAYDREAMING

A shaft of light peeled back my swollen eyelids. I was desperately tired and barely conscious. I did not want to wake. I moved forward and experienced considerable pain in my back. My neck and arms were powerless to move.

Struggling to focus, I gradually raised my body from the chair in which I had clearly lost consciousness. A strange feeling of insecurity came over me. Where was I? It was raining hard, but none of it seemed to settle on me.

The surroundings were unfamiliar. A fast-running river flowed alongside me, its water a luminous blue. Strange looking trees, neatly laid in rows, were shedding their leaves in unison from above. The crimson shapes danced their way to the water's surface. I was desperate to stretch my legs and alleviate the onset of cramp. I was clothed in a loose white robe, warm and soft to the touch. The light was intense. I heard nearby whispering. Easing my way back down into the chair, I breathed deeply. The whispering intensified, although it was impossible to understand what was being said. The voice grew louder and more confused. I slammed my eyes closed, grateful for the darkness. Then, the noise abated. There was a brief silence, then the voice returned, repeating over and over, "Are you awake?" "Are you awake?" "Are you awake?" Confused, I said, "Yes, yes I'm awake". My eyes opened and I found myself staring into a mirror, but the reflection was not mine. I reached out but failed to make contact. "Hello". Who's there?" I asked. There was no response. As I looked back into the mirror, I saw her face. There was no mistaking it - the image was that of the woman I had followed into the underground. I shouted out, "What's going on? Who are you? Where are you"?

Pages from a newspaper swept up on a sudden breeze. One floated down toward me. I leant forward and grabbed it. The headline read, 'Mystery woman found dead on the underground'. I read on. 'A woman was found dead on the London underground this morning. Police are anxious to speak to a man who was seen following her'.

The wind snatched up the paper. It flew high into the air and eventually faded from view. Was this the woman I had been following? Was I the man the police were looking for? I tried to stand, but the discomfort and the weight of my body dragged me down. I fell uncomfortably and began breathing erratically. In pain, I stretched my legs out in front of me and looked up. The sun's rays scattered my vision, and everything became obscured. "Are you awake. Are you awake?" I heard the voice again, repeatedly, this time in a softer but more urgent tone. "Yes, yes, I'm awake". I looked up and saw her in front of me. The sun pierced my eyes once more and I could see nothing but her silhouette. I asked her again, "Can you tell me who you are?" There was no response. I tried again. The shrillness of fleeing birds rang in my ears. The noises grew louder and more penetrating.

At that moment I woke with a start and found myself in the lap of a woman on the table next to me. I had fallen asleep and dropped off my chair.

Those close to my table laughed and ridiculed me as the waiter rushed toward the table to assist. Embarrassed, I collected my possessions, made my apologies, quickly paid the bill, and exited the building.

Outside, I hurriedly dressed to avoid the chill. I glanced at my watch I had less than fifteen minutes to get to Waterloo station if I were to catch a train to the West Country. I was attending an antique auction that evening. I took a taxi from Charing Cross.

My driver was a man in his mid-fifties, slightly balding and overweight, with a resigned, expressionless look on his face. I mentioned I was in a hurry to catch a train from Waterloo, laying emphasis on the word *hurry*. I hoped it would spur him on to get there as quickly as possible. It did not have the desired effect. After a brief silence, he began to recount how a friend, a fellow taxi driver that had spent thirty years in the job, had died prematurely of a heart attack. His tale was well rehearsed. At the beginning and end of each sentence, he glanced at me in the rear-view mirror for a reaction. I nodded at appropriate moments in the dialogue to convey the most basic of empathy, but my mind was focused on catching the train. At any other time, he would have had my full and undivided attention, but not that day. I sat back resigned to my fate. It seemed to take an undue amount of time to get there, the undesired but inevitable effect of clockwatching. When we finally arrived at Waterloo, I paid the fare and made my way to the concourse.

My train was running forty minutes late. The memory of the taxi driver and his story vanished into thin air. I continued to search the screen for confirmation of the delay. Satisfied, I turned and headed toward the nearest café. In recent years, a profound change had taken place in the hospitality sector, especially within the hot drinks industry. The everyday tea, instant coffee, and hot chocolate had been replaced by an exotic array of liquid consumables, many of which were impossible to pronounce. Off-hand waitresses had been replaced by smartly dressed and very attentive baristas. I *poured* over the menu for some time and ordered something I hoped would resemble coffee. It was handed to me in a vase. I transported it to the only vacant table in the corner next to the window, a position I felt comfortable with.

The couple sitting at the table opposite were clearly about to go their separate ways. Holding hands across the table, their dewy eyes were filled with emotion. On several occasions, I attempted to borrow a teaspoon but without success. He nervously stroked her hand and in response, she would gently touch his face. They were determined to make the most of their brief time together.

The café was heaving with people. The coffee machine performed its ritualistic act and the clatter of cups and saucers mingled with a thousand other noises that blended like a chaotic West End musical. Staffed hummed messages to each other and their customers, unaware that they were *the cast* providing life's dialogue.

The couple were now making repeated, urgent commitments to each other, finally faced with the moment of going their separate ways. They simultaneously checked their watches, wishing time would stand still. Holding hands, she skirted past my chair as he struggled precariously with her luggage. I watched as they slowly weaved their way across the concourse toward platform 9. He put the luggage down and they held each other tightly. The physical contact was only interrupted as they prized themselves apart to stare into each other's eyes.

They embraced again before she picked up her suitcase and bag, took a long, lasting look at him, and finally, without turning back, walked from his view. He stood there quite still, just staring ahead. I caught a last glimpse of her as she hurriedly boarded the train: destination, Weymouth. He turned and walked back in my direction. His head was bowed, his mind no doubt replaying the moments leading up to their parting. He walked past the window and then he, too, disappeared from my view. A brief separation, or a new chapter? I wondered to myself. Perhaps they would never see each other again?

A late middle-aged woman, best described as dowdy, grunted at me, clearly irritated that I was sprawled across the gangway, preventing her from sitting at the only vacant table. I appreciated her plight and offered a genuine and humble apology. It was met with stony silence. I had hoped for a smile or a simple acknowledgement, but she was having none of it. I wondered what had happened to those black-and-white movie days, when civility seemed to be the rule rather than the exception? That bygone era when men were portrayed as gentlemen and ladies respected as the gentler sex. Gentlemen opened doors for ladies and the ladies simply knew they would. A certain kind of romanticism, dignity, and respect were captured in those films I remembered so fondly. People knew what was assumed of them and self-discipline was the expected norm. Boundaries were clearly defined, and not to be crossed. It was a society where hierarchical structures meant everything, although aspiration was quelled in the lower classes, creating a different kind of divided society than we experience now. It was a system riddled with upper class self-indulgence, and lower-class deprivation and oppression at its worst. But I found watching those movies provided a certain security or reassurance that human beings were able to be respectful and civil to each, no matter how far from reality the depictions were. The films conjured up a social structure that I thought compared well against modern society, where it really is dog eat dog, and where old ladies with arthritic limbs are left stranded for what must seem like hours at supermarket doorways, waiting for someone, just anyone with a modicum of compassion, to hold open the door long enough for them to limp through. What new, more liberal revelations would confront us in the future, I wondered to myself?

The remains of the milk at the bottom of my coffee cup had dried into a congealed stain. It was time to leave and catch my train.

CHAPTER THREE - CHILDHOOD

REFLECTIONS

The countryside sped past as though it were being sucked into a vacuum cleaner. Land as far as the eye could see was so very green and lush, and the surroundings lay sodden. After the heaviest rainfall for over two hundred years, large sections of the countryside were now submerged in several feet of water, creating new streams and lakes in which huge numbers of wading birds had taken up residence. Much of the area had been lost to the floods.

Isolated farmhouses were dotted across the landscape like tiny, majestic islands cut off from the rest of humanity. What had originally been a country lane here, or a hedgerow there, now provided a haven for waterfowl. The minutes led to hours, and the hours filled my mind with childhood memories of summer holidays and what had seemed like great distances travelled. Car and train journeys in those days were a real treat, especially to the seaside or to see my parents' elderly relatives and friends. We lived in tight communities and shared in each other's experiences. It was only at holiday time did we stay away from home; the rest of the time, life was predictable but secure. As young children, we derived immense pleasure from exploring the local environment, acquiring an intimate knowledge of the trees, hedgerows, and animals that would regularly visit our hideouts. It was a carefree existence, but sadly one that I knew would never be experienced by the children of future generations.

At the age of eight or nine, we would disappear at weekends from dawn to dusk, without the need for parental supervision. We would roam the meadows and woodlands for miles around our village. We would invent characters for ourselves, often cowboys, and would play out the endless sequels of an ever-evolving storyline. As we got older, our childhood games matured and took on a new dimension. The herd instinct took over and gangs were formed. There would always be a leader, often the child most feared. The bullies would always find sustenance in gang life.

One boy, Greg, was particularly tough, ruthless, and unforgiving. Every gang member had to fall in line. To be cast out under any circumstances was something to be avoided. The fear of isolation from friends during the summer months was enough to bond the gang members together in all they did. New members were subjected to a ritualistic initiation that had been painstakingly devised for them. Thankfully, serious injuries were rare.

One ritual was to steal apples from the garden of Mr. Richards. The challenge was to collect as least one apple or pear for each gang member. Mr. Richards spent an awful lot of time in his garden. He was retired, in his late fifties and quite stocky, and he had little time for children. He had a temper, which he exercised on a regular basis. He was agile and few boys were able to outpace him. He had encountered gang members sufficiently often to know how to out-fox them. He knew every possible entry and exit point to the garden, and the quickest way of intercepting his target. This was no game for him. It was trespassing on his private property. When an intruder was apprehended, he would drag them to the local police station a few streets away. This was always followed by a visit to the boys' parents that evening.

Passing the initiation test demanded a great deal of courage, determination, and agility to avoid capture. It seemed innocent enough to me now, but Mr. Richards would surely tell a different story if he were still alive. The final, most dangerous task was to climb on the roof of a disused sawmill and run the full distance from one end to the other in an impossible pre-set time. It was a precarious journey of some 30 yards. The roof itself had suffered the indignity of many a boy sprinting across its beams and was littered with gaping holes, some six feet in width. If you failed to negotiate the course, the drop was about twenty feet - enough to break every bone in your body. On occasion, some were broken, but the cause of such incidents was concealed from parents at all costs.

Our exploits were finally curtailed when notices were posted in the yard, announcing the buildings were to be demolished to make way for a new housing estate. When the day arrived, heavy, demonic cranes were unloaded onto the site and the work began. For a few weeks as demolition got under way, we passed the time watching their every movement from concealed vantage points. Of course, knowing every inch of the yard, we were able to enter unseen and remain there for hours. Then, when boredom would finally take over, we could make our exit without trace. Eventually, every nook and cranny and every hideout had been flattened.

It was an emotional and exciting spectacle at the time, although none of us was prepared to admit it. It also marked the end of an era for the gang. In the weeks and months that followed, we seldom met up and eventually, we drifted apart. Some years later, I met Greg by accident. It proved to be an uncomfortable experience.

CHAPTER FOUR - THE TRAIN JOURNEY THAT CHANGED MY LIFE

I fell into a deep sleep. An hour passed until the train stopped abruptly at the next station and I awoke. Passengers shuffled about collecting their possessions and departed. Few were left in my carriage aside of a mother trying to occupy a crying baby.

In no time at all, we were on our way again. I sat back and peered out of the window. As the train gained pace, it reminded me of the days of steam, when one would sit and listen for the clatter of the wheels against intersection points in the track. It had a sleepy, soporific effect. But with the introduction of diesel and electric trains, the clatter had gone.

A tall, slim, fair-haired soldier sat opposite me and nodded. I nodded back and smiled. He hauled his kit bag and two battered suitcases onto the luggage rack above him. I wondered how on earth he was able to carry them on his own. He took off his overcoat and cap, placed them on top of the cases and sat down. I had always tried to engage in conversation with people on trains, although today it was considered an intrusion. After a brief silence, we spoke. He wasted no time. He was eager to tell me he was returning to barracks after leave, and judging by his tone, he was doing so reluctantly. He had been visiting his family and girlfriend in Hampshire. I quickly discovered he found their company more enjoyable than army life. He was stationed at Headquarters, South West, in Tidworth.

Before joining the forces, he had met his girlfriend at the local bank, where they worked together. His description of her was kind, slender, dark haired and with a *forgiving personality.* An odd description, I thought at the time. I listened attentively to him for some minutes, during which he seemed not to draw breath. His facial expressions and tone suggested few people gave him the time, and he was grateful for the attention. During the next hour, I was to discover a great deal about this highly intelligent and sensitive young man. He would reveal intimate details about his life that ordinarily would only be confided to the closest of family and friends. On this day, however, he had chosen me, a stranger on a train, to unburden his troubled mind. I felt privileged he had done so. His father had also been in the military, as his father had been before him. This was a family steeped in military history at the highest of ranks. It was expected that future generations would automatically follow in the tradition.

Peter, as I came to know him, had grown up with a father who was not an easy man to live with. A strong disciplinarian, the children lived in constant fear of verbal abuse and beatings. His mother protected the children as best she could but was also subjected to his father's *style of family management*. There were four children and Peter was the eldest. Unlike his father, he had a more gentle and sensitive disposition and did all he could to shield his mother and siblings from his tyrannical ways. In doing so, he often came under the greatest attack and recounted many occasions when he would be beaten for what seemed like hours, defending someone else's supposed misdemeanor.

Despite his experiences being so graphically portrayed, he appeared to bear no hatred for his father. It was clear that he was desperate for his affection but had received none. An overwhelming sense of sadness consumed him as he grew up. He believed it would be impossible to reconcile their relationship before his father died, and as it transpired, he was right. He had died in action and was awarded the military cross. Unlike him, his brothers and sister possessed a hatred for him that they had never forgiven. His mother was unable to recover from years of mental torment. She died too, unable to identify any of her children.

I was spellbound and visibly moved by his story. On several occasions, I was conscious that tears were welling up in my eyes and making moves to flood down my cheeks. He was sensitive to my dilemma and looked away on occasion, giving me time to wipe them dry and compose myself before looking back. Not for one moment did he deviate from telling his story. It was as if he sensed this was the last opportunity to do so. It mattered little to him that I was a stranger. He had found another human being willing to listen, and that was enough for him. I was still engrossed in his story when a second man joined us in the carriage, and all fell silent. He looked at both of us but focused his attention mainly on Peter. He began reading a newspaper. I sensed that the two men knew each other. There was an atmosphere that was unhealthy. Having listened to Peter for some time, I wanted to reassure him about his future. I was keen that the conversation did not end with the arrival of the stranger. I uttered something that seemed totally inadequate at the time. Politely, he acknowledged me, but then looked down at the floor. All further communication ceased as he sat uncomfortably in his seat. The stranger occasionally glanced at me over the top of his newspaper but said nothing.

As the train slowed in anticipation of arriving at the next station, I was convinced that Peter would make a move to leave the carriage. Eventually, we drew to a standstill. Both men remained in their seats for a moment, and then, as I thought, Peter rose purposefully from his seat and gathered his belongings. He turned to face me for the last time, smiled awkwardly, and without a word, bundled his bags out of the carriage and onto the platform. I saw him grab them hurriedly as he rushed in the direction of the exit.

The other man, who had been motionless until now, put his newspaper down. He, too, disembarked the train. I looked through the window and watched the man follow him. Both disappeared from my view. I puzzled over what I had seen but my musings were cut abruptly short when I heard a solitary round of gunshot. I immediately feared the worst. Had Peter been shot? Was he dead?

I looked toward the exit but saw nothing. I grabbed my belongings and attempted to get off the train, but it was too late. I could do nothing. I punched the window with my fist in sheer frustration. I tried to look beyond the platform exit as we passed. The next station was twenty minutes away. At that moment I decided I had to abandon my visit to the auction, disembark the train there and return to discover what had happened. The journey to the next station seemed to creep by. When the train finally stopped, I grabbed my bag and jumped onto the platform. Even if I managed to catch a train straight away, it would be almost an hour after the incident before I would be back at the station. So much would have happened. A train was due at any moment. I kept seeing Peter's face as he left the carriage. I climbed aboard as soon as it arrived. It was full - standing room only. After what seemed like an age, the guard blew the whistle and we pulled away. Slowly but surely, we inched our way out of the station and began increasing speed. I was unable to concentrate on anything other than the shooting. Was Peter dead or had he just been wounded? I found myself ignoring an elderly woman repeatedly asking to pass me. I was lost in my thoughts, so much so that I was surprised when I looked up to see that the train was coming into the station.

With both feet firmly on the platform, I threw my bag across my shoulder and moved swiftly toward the exit. There were a lot of people queuing at the gate and I could see a policeman's helmet bobbing about at the back of the group. I pushed forward and tried to speak to him. He ignored me. Another passenger standing at my side told me the news that a man had been shot dead and his assailant had run off in the direction of woodland that ran adjacent to the station. My worst fears had come true. Now I was here, I had to investigate further. I waited for the policeman to turn away, hauled myself up onto the barrier, and leapt over. I slipped on the polished floor but managed to scramble out of sight, toward the ticket office.

As I approached, several people were in a circle talking. I proceeded more slowly and saw four policemen standing close to a body that was covered with a grey blanket. I walked toward them. There were pools of blood seeping from the body. It had to be Peter. I stopped in front of them. "Do you know him?" Was he a relative or close friend?" a policeman asked. "I met him on the train," I replied. I was shaking and visibly distressed. One policeman led me to a nearby seat, out of sight of the corpse. For ten minutes, I was questioned about the man I had met on the train. I told them all I knew; the conversation we had, how moved I had been to hear about his childhood and his father's heavy hand. I recalled the other man, the murderer, joining us in the carriage and how the atmosphere had instantly changed. I went on to explain that Peter had left the carriage hurriedly, and how the man had followed him until I heard the shot. They seemed genuinely sympathetic, making notes throughout. What puzzled them was why I kept referring to Peter as a *young man*. I was asked to identify the body, something I dreaded. As they pulled the blanket back, they revealed the face of the dead man.

The body was that of the man that followed Peter off the train. It all seemed so unreal. I learned that eyewitnesses said the man I described as Peter had cold bloodedly waited for him to arrive at the barrier, then, pulled out a gun and shot him at point blank range, before running away from the station toward the woodland. He had been in an emotional state when he left the train, but I could not imagine him doing such a thing, even in desperation. I was asked to remain at the railway station to give a formal statement. I relived the encounter in my mind, trying to recollect the circumstances leading up to Peter's departure from the train, but I came up with no new revelations that made any sense. An ambulance arrived and took the body away. The police left the building. I wondered how long it would be before they came back to take my statement. The minutes passed and no one returned. I was anxious about Peter. The station exit was twenty feet away. I decided there was only one way of finding out what really happened. I had to find him.

CHAPTER FIVE – ON THE RUN

I walked quickly outside and into the cold air. A narrow pathway running parallel to the station exit seemed the best way to go. It was muddy underfoot, and the woods became dense as it led deeper into the undergrowth. I stopped for a moment. I needed a strategy if I had any hope of finding him. Far off in the distance, I could hear dogs barking and assumed they were the search party. It seemed odd that the pathway I had chosen had not been cordoned off. It was getting dark and I had no torch, nor did I know where I was heading. I was not dressed for a walk let alone a hike. What chance was there of finding him? What would I do if I did? The questions came in quick succession, but they were unaccompanied by any rational answers. An hour ago, I was on my way to an important antiques auction, hoping to acquire furniture for a client, now I was hunting for a murderer. It all seemed so surreal.

The sky eventually turned black and I was stumbling in the dark. I knew there was little I could do now. It made sense to find accommodation locally and return to London in the morning. That said, I could not bring myself to walk away and get on with my life knowing Peter was out there somewhere, probably in a highly stressed state. The distant dog barking had stopped and owls, ready for their night vigil, were making their presence known.

I had only ventured a short distance into the woods, but my return journey proved far more difficult to navigate. The thick mud stuck like glue to the bottom of my shoes and it was hard to walk. I tripped on a tree root and fell unceremoniously into a puddle at the side of the path. I lay there for some seconds, soaking up the content before getting to my feet. I felt wretched and irritated that I had chosen to leave the station. After a while, the pathway began to widen, and I knew I was close to the station. A streetlight became a visible target to aim for.

A shower of rain swept toward me. I took cover. I was out of breath, soaked, and caked in thick mud. The station was quiet as if nothing had happened. Suddenly, I felt a sharp prod in my back. Startled, I turned to discover Peter behind me. Without a word, he pushed me out of the lamplight into darkness. I was relieved but shocked to see him. "What on earth happened, Peter?" I asked. "I can't tell you here. We must go somewhere safe. The police are looking for me". That I knew.

We walked quickly away from the station, across the path that led to the woods and into open space. It was just possible to see our way. He held my arm tightly as if not to lose me. We walked for some minutes, the rain and wind howling around us. He seemed to know where he was going. A few allotments lay ahead. We scrambled over a small wire fence and jumped into a muddy ditch before stopping at a large wooden shed. He forced the door with his shoulder. Inside, he lit a paraffin lamp with matches he had found there. The light flickered as eerie shadows bounced around the room. The smell of paraffin reminded me of the days at the timber yard, when we had used an old heater in the winter to keep us warm. We were both exhausted from the trek and soaked to the bone. I slumped down onto a battered folding chair. "I had a feeling we would meet up again," he said. "What made you come back to the station?" I explained that I knew there was something sinister between him and the other man, and after they had left the train, I had watched them walk to the exit. Then, as the train had started to move, I had heard the gunshot. I assumed it was him on the receiving end of the bullet. It was then that I decided to return to find out what happened. "There aren't many people like you," he said. By now, he had dragged an old sofa toward the lamp and was sitting opposite me.

I returned to my interrogation. "What on earth happened, Peter?" He looked sheepishly at me, wondering if what he was about to say would shatter my view of him. His voice was shaky. "You remember me telling you about my girlfriend?" I nodded slowly. "Well, she's older than I led you to believe, and married to John Crawford, the man I shot. They have a young child. He was cold and possessive, and violent towards her. She felt trapped and imprisoned in the relationship and needed to escape. We met at the bank where we worked, and I immediately fell in love with her. I know it sounds stupid now, but I did. At first, she rejected me, but I begged her to see me. I knew she was married but I just wanted her, to be with her. We had snatched moments of time together, meeting where we would not be seen. I knew we were living dangerously but I did not care about the consequences. After a while, we started meeting for longer periods. Often, she was able to leave her son with a friend when we were together. Then, we started meeting at her house. I would sneak in through the back gate. We had never made love together until that first day I went to the house."

His voice began to shake with emotion. It was difficult for him to continue. He paused, dropped his head, and wept uncontrollably. His hands covered his face as tears seeped through his fingers and dripped to the floor. The light from the lamp danced in the draught, creating obscure images on the ceiling and walls. He regained his composure, describing the passion they had for each other. Then, he cleared his throat, sat upright, and returned to what had happened that fateful day at her house.

"We didn't hear him until it was too late. He had come home early from work. Mary and I were in bed together. It was only when the stairs creaked on the landing, we knew someone was about to enter the bedroom. I panicked and leapt out of bed. The bedroom window was open, and I managed to get onto the corrugated roof of an outbuilding that adjoined the house and scramble away before he was able to grab me. I was almost naked. My clothes were left sprawled on the floor at the side of the bed. I ran away like a wounded dog. I could only think of Mary and the consequences she faced. I was just able to catch a glimpse of him in the window as I disappeared from the scene. Selfishly, I wondered if he got a good view of me and would be able to identify me if he saw me again. For weeks, I thought of nothing but Mary, but feared making contact. Sometime later, friends discovered that he had beaten her, but she refused to tell him anything about me. Eventually, though, she had no option. He said he would hunt me down and kill me. This was almost three months ago, and I haven't seen or heard from her since".

I was in no position to pass moral judgment. What struck me more than anything was the irony of the situation he found himself in. He and his family had suffered at the hands of their father when they were young, and he was only too aware of the pain that the experience had caused. Mary and her children, too, had been subjected to a similar brutality, but this time, the burden of guilt was quite rightly resting on his shoulders for persuading a married woman into a relationship. Despite this, I still believed Peter was not without integrity. Love knows no bounds, and the minds of those consumed by love can work in irrational, if not dangerous ways.

By now, we were both shivering. The light from the wick weakened as the paraffin ran low. There was a silence as I struggled to find the right words to support him. I decided to change the subject to address our more immediate needs as the glow from the lamp dimmed further. "How did you find this place?" I asked.

"I fled the station, not knowing where to go, and stumbled across it. I had to find somewhere to hide and it was easy to get in. I stayed for a few minutes, but I was confused about what to do. I decided there was no point in trying to run away so I returned to the station with the intention of giving myself up. Then, I came across you." "So why did you lead me away from the station and come back here?" I asked. "Seeing you gave me hope. In a split second, I knew that by giving myself up, I would never see Mary again. I would likely go to prison and my life would be over. I just could not bear to think what it would be like". "I know it's a lot to ask but can you help me?". I chose not to answer.

The wick consumed its last drop of paraffin. The flame died in an instant and darkness descended upon us. My eyes adjusted to a faint beam of light entering the window, illuminating Peter's face. "So, what should you do now, Peter?" He looked up and shrugged. "I don't know, I just don't know. I would like to go back and find Mary, but I know that would be impossible".

It was getting late and the temperature was dropping. I had to decide a course of action that would conceal him for the time being. I was getting embroiled in his drama when I should be heading back to London. I could not abandon him. We needed more adequate shelter, and we needed to eat. I could see Peter expected me to take the initiative. I had assumed the role of surrogate father and with it, the responsibility of deciding what to do next. His life was in my hands, at least that was how it seemed. Instinctively, I knew he should give himself up, but first we had to prepare him for what might lay ahead.

I was unfamiliar with the area, so I had no idea where we could stay. Earlier in the woods, I had fallen into a ditch and my clothes were caked in mud as if I had spent time in the trenches. We made for the door and walked out into the rain, which took no pity on us. Peter had lost his suitcases and was now travelling light. My briefcase had also disappeared. Reluctant to return to the station just in case we ran into the police, we headed across the allotments toward a housing estate. The thick mud that clung to our shoes made it impossible to move at pace.

We remained silent until we reached the edge of the allotments. Once there, we climbed over an unsteady wire fence and I tore my trousers, grazing my leg. I could not remember a time in my adult life when I felt so wretched. We were cold, wet, muddy, homeless, hungry, and fugitives to boot - at least, Peter was. And now, I was his accomplice. The chances of finding any hostelry that would take us in looking like we did was remote, but we had to try and find somewhere. We walked for over an hour through the estate to a main road. The options were to seek a bed locally or hitch a lift to the next town. The decision was an easy one. With Peter on the run, it made sense to get as far away as we reasonably could.

We found a streetlight for illumination and remembering my student days, I stood at the side of the road with my thumb held high. Before long, a truck stopped and we both clambered aboard. "Where are you heading?" I asked. "Dover. And you?" The question was simple enough, the answer a little more difficult to provide. "Oh, just to the next town would be fine. We're looking for somewhere to stay for the night." He dropped us twenty minutes later at a trucker's café that had accommodation. According to him, "The beds are comfortable and clean, the food's the best in miles, and the landlady is very accommodating!" I thought better than seek clarification on the meaning of his latter remark.

We climbed out of the truck, said goodbye to our driver, and hurried into the shack and out of the rain. Debbie, the landlady, greeted us as if we were long lost cousins. The place was deserted. It was sparsely furnished with worn carpets and pictures of the Queen Mother and film stars adorning the cracked walls. Dusty lightbulbs hung ungracefully from the ceiling. The warmth of the room was extremely welcoming and Debbie's rotund, beaming face was full of excitement. "Are you looking for rooms?" "Yes. And a good meal if that's OK?" "That's what we're here for, duck". I wondered what she thought of the two forlorn characters standing before her. To her, though, our appearances did not seem to matter. The thought of the till being exercised in the morning was good enough for her.

We were shown our rooms, exchanging idle conversation as we walked. We were both very hungry and arranged to meet back in the café as soon as practically possible, giving us enough time to have baths and smarten up as best we could. I cannot describe the pleasure of seeing a bed that would be mine for the night, and the bath, though heavily stained, was welcoming beyond description.

It took no time for me to strip naked and submerge myself in the hot water. It must be one of the most wonderful experiences a human being can have. Too tired to take cleaning myself too seriously, I just lay there, moving occasionally to allow the hot water to rush over me. I reflected on the last few hours and contemplated the immediate future. Peter needed to give himself up. There was no alternative. It seemed clear to me that after breakfast in the morning, we should make our way to the nearest police station and the deed would be done and I could return to normality. But I feared for his future. Despite the facts of the situation, shooting a man in cold blood was murder, and at best, he would face a lengthy prison sentence. At worst, he would probably get life. The thought of any man being incarcerated for life sent a shiver down my spine. He was not a murderer, at least not as one would imagine a murderer to be. He was a sensitive and naive young man who had just happened to get involved in an unfortunate affair that had led to a tragic conclusion. As the bath water chilled, I knew I had to stand by him whatever the circumstances. Other than the business which Mandy my assistant could run for me, I had no other immediate or significant commitments to attend to, so I decided that I would do what I could for him. I washed the mud off my legs and climbed out of the tub. Dressing in damp, dirty clothes was the last thing I wanted to do, but there was no alternative. The pangs of hunger returned as dinner awaited.

Peter was already sat down in the café, thumbing through the menu. The room was still deserted. He looked tired, as I am sure I did, and aside from a clean face, he looked disheveled. His muddy and sodden clothes hung off him, as did mine.

The quietness of the café itself was far removed from the din in the kitchen, where Debbie was singing along to the local radio station on full volume. "Good soak?" I asked. "It was great. The problem was getting back into these damp clothes." I knew the feeling.

I looked at the menu. Everything seemed so appealing. Fried this and fried that. I had always tried to avoid fatty foods, but now, it did not seem to matter in the least. We were both hungry and anything would do. Debbie made a grand entrance. "Rooms okay, gents?" We responded simultaneously, "Great thanks." "What are you having then?" Peter went first and ordered enough for three people. I, too, went a little overboard. "Double egg, large portion of chips, two sausages, bacon, tomatoes, mushrooms, fried bread, black pudding, two slices of toast, and a pot of tea." "You're hungry then!" she chuckled.

We gorged ourselves, cleaning our plates until they sparkled. We needed to discuss the next move, but Peter managed to steer clear of the subject for a good hour, as Debbie kept popping in and out to see if we needed anything. Other than us, the café remained deserted as the wind and rain beat a rhythmic tune on the corrugated roof above us. Finally, I broached the subject. "Given any more thought to what you should do next?"

It was clear from the look on his face that he had expected me to raise the subject and had duly prepared his answer. "Yes. I want to contact Mary. I thought if I were to make my way back, I could persuade her to run away with me. I am grateful for all the help you have given me, and for… well… just believing in me. But I have to see her again and explain what happened." I could tell by his expression that my reaction was of little consequence; he had made up his mind. I tried anyway. "It won't work, you know. You need to give yourself up. You can't live your life on the run, and what if Mary decides after what happened that she wants nothing to do with you?" "She won't, I just know it," he quickly retorted. The conversation continued in this way for a while, but it was clear that nothing I could possibly say would dissuade him from his plan to see Mary. I craved my warm bed and a good night's sleep. We agreed to meet for breakfast at 8.00 am.

I was extremely tired, but sleep eluded me for thinking about Peter's future and what was in store for him. I looked at my watch. It was almost 4.00 am. I lay there, hoping to get a little extra sleep before breakfast. Thankfully, luck was on my side.

CHAPTER SIX - A NEED FOR

DECISIONS

There was an insistent knock at the door. It was Peter. By the time I had dragged myself out of bed and made my way to the café, he was almost through eating. It was quite busy with truck drivers. A plume of smoke cloaked the room. Somehow, the law on *not smoking* inside cafés was yet to reach Debbie's establishment. At first, we indulged in idle conversation. It was obvious Peter was expecting me to try again to persuade him to another course of action. Instead, I told him about my life and the challenges I had faced over the years. I could see he was intrigued. Simple explanations failed to quench his thirst. Question upon question rained down upon me as the café got busier.

It was almost nine thirty. I was about to return to the central issue of Peter's plans, when out of the blue he raised the subject of his own accord, his statement taking me by surprise. "By the way, I've changed my mind. I *am* going to give myself up. You were right". He looked at me, seeking approval. I was delighted and saddened by the news.

It was the right thing to do and there was no alternative, but I dreaded the thought of him spending so many futile years behind bars. We discussed his decision. I said I respected his integrity and courage and would support him as best I could. The reality was he had little hope of avoiding a lengthy prison sentence. I reassured him I would act as a character witness, but in truth, I knew so little about him, apart from the conversation on the train. I could not fabricate a story to protect him, nor would he expect me to do so. Suddenly, his dilemma hit home, and he went quiet.

We sat in awkward silence until we returned to our respective rooms to pick up our few belongings. We agreed to meet in the car park ten minutes later. He glanced at me for a split second. I could tell by his facial expression that the gravity of the situation had dawned on him. I waited for almost twenty minutes in the car park, but he failed to show. In a strange way, I was not surprised.

I went to his room and found the door ajar. I walked in, not wanting to intrude but with every expectation that the room would be empty. My instinct was right. He had gone, save a note left on the bed addressed to me.

"You have been a real friend. Apart from what is left of my family I cannot imagine anyone doing what you have done for me. I do not know how I got into this mess, but here I am. I know I should give myself up, and I know you would support me as best you could, but the thought of going to prison for the rest of my life is just too much to come to terms with. I have decided to go into hiding until everyone forgets all about me. It is the only chance I have. I would appreciate it if you would not tell the police anything about me for at least a day or two. If you feel you must, of course, I will understand. I really hope we will meet again in the future under better circumstances. Peter."

I read the note several times. Even when you are expecting something like this to happen, it takes time to hit home. He was a very worried young man and anyone in his position would feel scared. Who could blame him for wanting to disappear, rather than face up to his responsibilities, but what future would he have on the run? As for reporting him, the thought would never have entered my head. Once again, I found myself totally embroiled in this young man's life. How could I abandon him? Left to his own devices, he would be picked up in no time; at least, that was my assessment.

There were a few options open to me and no time to waste. I knew I had to find him. I figured that he would attempt to hitch a lift, but not too close to the café, perhaps a mile or so down the road. But in which direction? It seemed sensible to assume that he would continue to follow the same direction we had been taking before we were dropped off at the café. Or would he? He may well have decided to go in the opposite direction to throw me off the scent. I weighed up the options. In his state of mind, he would not be thinking logically. I made for the car park, then the main road. He was nowhere to be seen. Peter had either hitched a lift or decided to leave the main road and headed across farmland. I thought it likely that he would choose the former.

I started walking in the direction we had headed the day before, constantly listening out for vehicles approaching to hitch a lift. The bath I had had the previous evening cleansed me, but my clothes were still uncomfortably stiff.

In the distance behind me, I heard a truck approaching and turned to attract the driver's attention. I raised my thumb in anticipation. I could tell by the engine noise that it was slowing down and moments later, I was climbing aboard. I had no idea where we were heading. I tried to explain to the driver that I was looking out for someone, but he understood little English. The registration plates on the vehicle were Polish. I had the bizarre experience of sitting in the offside front seat as though I were driving this ten-ton monster. Credit where credit is due, he tried desperately to communicate with me, but I struggled to understand him. I was quick to accept that my Polish was non-existent. He was middle-aged, bald, and overweight. I sensed he had enjoyed many a hearty English breakfast. A cigarette was glued to his lips. He drew breath and exhaled the smoke through his nose. His chest wheezed and rattled as he did. He blurted out odd incomprehensible words thinking I should understand, but I did not. He was friendly enough. He chuckled to himself as though I had amused him in some way, but there was nothing I said that could be interpreted in any language as humorous. Perhaps something was lost in translation?

We had been driving for about twenty minutes and I was already beginning to think tracking Peter down was like finding a needle in a haystack. When my companion said he was stopping at the next roadside café for a break, I was relieved. It was a possibility, albeit remote, that Peter had found a lift and stopped at the same spot. We drove into the car park. The air brakes exhaled. Fifteen or more trucks were parked up alongside us. The driver motioned to me, expecting me to join him, but I waved him on, giving me time to look around. If I had any chance of finding Peter, this was where I felt he would be. I entered the café. The place was noisy. Fruit machines were working overtime as the melodic tones of the Rolling Stones singing 'Jumping Jack Flash' belted out from the jukebox. Smoke belched from every corner of the room. There was no sign of Peter. I wondered what to do next.

I headed back to the truck twenty minutes later, sensing it was pointless to continue further. The chance of finding him was nigh on impossible now, but I was wrong. He was standing right there, by a car door. Dodging past our truck, I ran straight toward him. He turned and saw me. He looked frightened, no doubt thinking that I had betrayed him and was accompanied by the police. I held out my hand and he warmly shook it.

My driver had got back into his truck and started the engine. He blasted his horn and waved at me. Peter planned to go across country so I signaled that I would be going on foot. He drove past us, out onto the open road, and disappeared in the distance. Before too long, Peter and I were heading south.

It was reminiscent of two days earlier. The mud clung to my shoes like syrup and my soaked trousers hugged my legs.

CHAPTER SEVEN - A NEW LIFE

IN WINCHESTER

Some days later, we arrived in Winchester, sixty miles south-west of London and 14 miles from the port of Southampton. The sun was shining.

I had lost my credit cards and any identification during my attempt to track Peter down. I was now forced to rely on the dwindling cash I had in my trouser pocket. Life prior to meeting Peter had been good, and I was grateful for the lifestyle I enjoyed. I was financially comfortable and wanted for nothing, but there was a lot missing in my life, not least of all seeing my children often enough. I had the business, close friends, the occasional girlfriend, and plenty of challenges to keep me focused, but it was not enough. Now though, despite the circumstances I found myself in, I felt strangely focused. Perhaps it was the adventurer in me? I knew I was attempting to pervert the course of justice by shielding Peter. Ostensibly, I was homeless, short of cash, and living like a vagrant - the last set of circumstances most people would feel at home with. But I did - at least for the time being.

We discussed Peter's plight at length. I agreed that for the time being, I would stay with him and we would take on assumed names. It would be impossible for Peter to join mainstream society. If he ever did it would come with its own challenges, not least of all, basic documentation to confirm his status. I knew that going to the police was not an option he wanted to pursue. Peter was confident he could adjust to a different life from the one he knew. Of course, for me, it would only be temporary. Whatever happened the future remained uncertain for him. What we both had was a determination and will to make it work for him. Our immediate need was to seek shelter for the night.

Winchester was once the capital of England and a stronghold of the Roman army. Our arrival in the city was less dramatic than the Roman's had been two thousand years ago, but nonetheless, having arrived, we decided it would be our own stronghold for the foreseeable future. We had presented ourselves as two affable *down and outs* and sought refuge in one of the many hostels for the homeless in the city. There were few comforts, but we were grateful for clean beds, good but basic food, and protection from the elements. In conversation, we uncovered a shared passion for jazz. Peter was reasonably accomplished with a guitar. I played the tenor sax. After two weeks of begging on the streets, which was a salutary experience, we were able to afford to buy both instruments in a local secondhand shop, and we were in business. I decided not to access my assets and cash fearing my new, temporary identity might be compromised. They would languish until the day I thought it was safe to use them. I had a lengthy conversation with Mandy and asked her to run my business back in London in my absence. I had to fabricate a story that sounded vaguely plausible, and she accepted it. She already had access to all aspects of buying, selling, administration, and finances. I felt guilty leaving her to it, especially having lied to her about my motives for doing so. However, I knew she would do a good job and I could trust her.

Busking for a living appealed to us both. We spent considerable time rehearsing our repertoire. We were quite good as a duo. The locals and tourists rewarded us well. On a good day, we would collect almost sixty pounds for our efforts. The weeks and months passed, and we slipped into our new identities with ease. Rarely did we talk about the past, preferring instead to focus on the present believing the future would take care of itself.

It was close to Christmas and the weather was deteriorating. We had lived in various abodes in the city and had become *local characters*. I am not sure what people really thought of us, but I am confident they saw us as *different* from the other homeless people that regularly sat begging on the streets. A cohort of about a dozen such people had a daily routine, it seemed, of going about their business until about 11.00 am, when they would disappear to the local pharmacy for their daily methadone fix. They would re-appear soon after midday on a high, carrying bottles of alcohol that they would then consume in the cathedral grounds until they were comatose. It was a wasted life for these young men. I wondered what had led to their dependency. Had they experienced brutal or deprived childhoods like Peter? Why had they chosen life on the streets and addiction, rather than working for a living to pay their way in life? These were questions I was not qualified to answer.

We were lucky enough to be offered accommodation by the local council, without the need for documentation. Our apartment in the city was on the ground floor of a small, discreetly positioned block which needed refurbishment. It had two small bedrooms, a bathroom, a living room-cum-kitchen, and the most spectacular views of the cathedral. On Sundays, the bells rang out and I looked forward to hearing them. They provided a sense of wellbeing and community spirit. Unfortunately, our regular source of income was cut short as Peter had been suffering from a lengthy cold which had turned to flu, meaning we had to give our performances a break. His mood swung wildly as he struggled to cope with the boredom of not getting out. He was miserable most of the time, and sometimes impossible to get on with. My own health and levels of fitness had suffered during those months, and occasionally, I seriously considered returning to my normal, comfortable life. I never let on to Peter that I felt this way.

Even when he got better, he was reluctant to leave the apartment and spent most of the days leading up to Christmas in bed. His moods had become intolerable. I could not bear to be around him, and he knew it. Every morning, I had to go out or go crazy. Most days, it was easy to occupy myself. One of my preferred haunts was an antiquarian bookshop tucked away in a small alley that ran parallel to the high street. Upon entering, a musty smell immediately hit the nostrils. It was a charming retreat full of the most wonderful leather-bound books. The owners, Andy and Rob were incredibly knowledgeable about their inventory that straddled three floors of a medieval building. Each floor was accessed by a narrow stairwell built much later in the building's history. The floors creaked under the weight of the books. The silence, apart from the odd cough or pages being turned, was a real treat. I rarely bought anything, but they were happy to engage in conversation with someone knowledgeable about *old books,* which of course I was.

We became quite good acquaintances, but I avoided talking about my life. It was too complicated. I am sure they thought me a little odd. My way of repaying their attention was buying cups of take away coffee from a café opposite, for which they seemed grateful. One day, I plucked up the courage to ask them if they wanted an assistant. A regular income would be handy, no matter how small, but I knew being paid legitimately through the books would create complications I could do without. They looked at each other, seeking guidance on what to say. Clearly, they did not need my help.

Sensitive to their plight, I suggested that if they did find themselves in a situation where they needed an extra pair of hands, to let me know. After all, I was in and out of the shop on a regular basis. Regretting making the request, I then smiled, said goodbye, and began to exit. Just then, though, Rob, one of the owners, responded positively. He explained that his wife had been seriously unwell, and they had thought of advertising for part-time help so he could spend more time at home while she recuperated. Just like that, I had a part time job. I would work on Wednesdays and Thursdays for the foreseeable future and Andy suggested they would discuss an hourly rate between them. I was delighted and agreed to start the following day.

I had a renewed purpose. It sounds pathetic, but this meant a lot to me. I needed to *do* something and what could be better than working in a bookshop? Not just any bookshop, but *this* book shop. I left with grin on my face, marching off to the café around the corner to celebrate.

I found it hard to sleep that night. I had mixed emotions. I was looking forward to my new job but had not mentioned my good fortune to Peter, knowing that he would sulk. I did not want an inquisition or to battle with him, nor did I feel should I have to. I had to keep reminding myself that I was not his keeper. Not his father. In fact, not even a family member, but a stranger that had done all he could to support another human being in need.

The new life I had adopted bore no resemblance to the life I had led before that fateful day on the train. Peter had forgotten that he was still a criminal. I hesitated to use the word *murderer,* because I genuinely believed it was not his true intention to shoot his girlfriend's husband. The truth was, though, that he did, and he remained a wanted man. Countless thousands, if not millions of people worldwide have committed unacceptable deeds. They could argue that their crimes had been committed under *special* circumstances, that there were plausible reasons for their transgressions, but sadly, that would not wash in a court of law. I knew Peter was one of them.

I had helped him during a crisis. I had given him hope when no one else was there to do so. I had become a surrogate father, but I was paying the price of becoming a prisoner in the friendship, not knowing when I might say or do something that would upset him. I questioned my rationale for staying. I could not contemplate living in such a negative environment for much longer. How long could I realistically expect to protect and shield Peter, and in doing so, trade my own future? I did not *owe* him anything.

I switched the kettle on. It was almost 5.00 am. My mind was buzzing. I made tea and sat at the table, wondering how to deal with the situation. Peter was constantly miserable. He lacked self-motivation. He struggled to get through the days and like a teenager, he demanded attention but rejected constructive advice. I finished my tea and made my way to the bathroom. I knew something had to change.

CHAPTER EIGHT - THE

BOOKSHOP

It was 8.30 am and I left for my first day at bookshop. I knew I would be early, but I used the excess time to browse through shop windows. Yesterday's joy had already turned to frustration as I had not come to a meaningful conclusion about what to do about Peter.

When I arrived, Andy was there to greet me with a cup of coffee and explain the workings of the shop. I learned that they acquired inventory in three ways. They bought from other reputable dealers, via house clearances (which were a regular source of interesting titles), and of course, auctions. This was all familiar territory to me, although Andy was unaware of my business activities in London. While they had an intimate knowledge of the inventory, there was little evidence of record keeping. I knew from experience that unless you were able to keep on top of administration through systems processes and procedures, the business was like a kite in the wind, blowing in all directions.

According to Andy, the business was financially sound, but they did not earn enough for both partners to work full time. Consequently, they both had part-time jobs to supplement their income. Rob gave English Literature classes at a local college and Andy taught piano to children after school. I felt confident that with better management and promotion of the bookshop, part-time working would be unnecessary for them. However, I knew it was neither my place nor was it wise for me to explain why. Fortunately, Andy asked little about me. I did not want to lie or fabricate stories about my past, or indeed the predicament I found myself in.

First, I had to acquaint myself with the range and diversity of titles, and the general layout of the shop. I was expected to do anything to help. I would serve customers and keep sales records. This amounted to scribbling the title and sale price on a sheet of paper. I was under strict instruction not to sell anything under list price. They did not want to be branded as *discounters*, a term that now pervaded the book trade. The thought of it made them feel uneasy. I found this policy quite refreshing. That said, their strategy for pricing was totally arbitrary, and not based on any retail markup formula I was familiar with. I felt my enthusiasm and excitement returning. Within an hour of walking through the door, Andy had left me to it and said he would return at 4.00 pm. Very few people came in during the morning, giving me time to better acquaint myself with the business.

It was just after 11.00 am when I found myself in the basement of the building: *the cellar.* A heavy musty smell verging on the unpleasant was suspended in the air. I found the light switch, but it failed to work. I had seen a torch in an upstairs draw, so I went to fetch it. Returning, I shone a beam around the room. It was larger than I had imagined, with a low and uneven ceiling. It resembled an ancient prison cell, dingy damp and sinister. Rubbish was strewn everywhere. Cardboard, rags, plastic sheeting, bottles, and odd bits of furniture that had served a purpose in the distant past waited to be ceremonially dumped. Dirty blankets coated in layers of dust partly covered rubbish I could not fully see underneath, and cobwebs were everywhere.

An old bookcase which housed an assortment of old papers and magazines and several hardback books stood in a corner. One newspaper I picked up was dated Wednesday 19th January 1944. The headline read, *'British bombers conducted their heaviest raid on Berlin yet, dropping 2,300 tons of bombs in just over half an hour. German submarine U-641 was depth charged and sunk in the Atlantic Ocean by the British corvette Violet'.*

I picked up a book and blew dust off the cover. 'A Christmas Carol by Charles Dickens'. It was dated 1843. It looked to be a first edition in almost mint condition. Why was it left here in such a forlorn state and not on sale in the shop? I picked up another and brushed off the dust. The cover itself was torn in several places. 'The Turn of the Screw' by Henry James. 1898. There were other titles that appeared to be first editions, too, just left unappreciated, quietly accumulating dust and dampness.

The building the bookshop occupied was first built in the late 15th century. A plaque on the outside of the building proudly announced the fact. Cellars tend to have a foreboding feel about them. Dark, damp, cramped, and occupied by spiders, mice, and mites finding ways to survive undisturbed. This cellar was no different, except for one thing. I did not believe in ghosts and fairy stories, nor was I a religious man, but I knew that something had happened in this cellar. I had an odd feeling about it.

I poked around for long enough before returning to the shop. I considered whether I should ask Andy or Rob about the books I had discovered but decided against it. It was not my place to be poking around in the first place. The doorbell rang sharply, prizing me from my thoughts. It was the postman. He handed me four letters that appeared to be junk mail or bills, and a small parcel. It was almost certainly a book Rob had ordered. It was nearly 4.00 pm and Andy was due back. I had enjoyed an interesting day but had little to report in terms of book sales. There was clearly so much they could do to promote their investment in the business, but I sensed that promotion, marketing, and indeed finance matters did not come naturally to them. 4.00 pm came and went but there was no sign of Andy. I wandered around the shop, trying to remember on which floor individual book categories were situated, testing myself as I went.

The clock by the entrance door chimed five times. Andy was an hour late. I was in no hurry to leave. After all, I would only have to contend with Peter when I returned to the apartment. Who knows what kind of mood he would be in? That said, I was tired - the kind of tiredness one feels when lacking exercise. I decided whatever time he returned I would run rather than walk back to the flat. It was 6.20 pm when Andy finally walked through the door. He had been held up in traffic and was pleasantly surprised to see me. We talked for ten minutes before I left and started the run.

When I got back, Peter was in his dressing gown and slumped on the sofa watching TV. During the run, I had decided I would confront him about his moods and tell him about my job. We talked for over an hour and he was surprisingly apologetic. He acknowledged he had become withdrawn after having the flu and was feeling despondent about life. He could not stop thinking about Mary and wondered what the future held in store for him. I accepted his apology and reminded him that he was in control of his own destiny. Life could be a lot worse and he had to make the most of it or choose a different path.

I told him about my job at the bookshop, expecting a negative reaction, but he seemed genuinely pleased for me. Despite the countless hours we had spent together since meeting, he knew little about me and my past, my business, and my interests other than the brief conversation we had had in Debbie's café months earlier. Our conversations had invariably been about him. Clearly, this conversation had a positive effect on him. He admitted it was unfair on me and, indeed, on him to continue in this malaise. He got dressed and went for a walk, saying he would bring back a takeaway. We ate later. Afterwards, Peter stayed up and I went to bed. I spent the night thinking about the bookshop; the various book categories, how I could add value to the business, and of course, the cellar.

The following morning, I left for the bookshop without breakfast. Peter, as far as I could make out, was still in bed. It was raining and people hurried from their cars, heading to work or to go shopping. I was in a good mood. Clearing the air with Peter yesterday evening had been the right thing to do. I had taken a risk in telling him about his attitude, but it had seemed to work. Time would tell if he would maintain his new sense of purpose. For me, the commitment made to support Peter through his ordeal would be maintained for the time being, but a time was nearing when he would need to create a life for himself. My role as surrogate father was coming to an end. I needed my own life back.

The rain continued. I arrived at the bookshop as Andy was unloading books from his car, which he had acquired at auction. I helped him in with the stock. We chatted for a while. Andy had more of a passion for old books than Rob. He became animated when he talked about the subject. I offered to go and fetch coffee, he stayed for a couple of hours, then left me on my own again. We had not seen a browser, let alone a customer in all that time. I enjoyed being at the shop. I relished the opportunity to ferret around and occasionally sit down and engross myself in a book. Apart from the faint droning of traffic, the place was silent. The musty, damp air from the cellar permeated every level of the building. Some of the older titles on the shelves had been exposed to the elements for some years and had suffered. Pages had yellowed and damp spots had appeared, which undermined their value - if they had any to speak of in the first place. There was no heat in the building, other than an electric bar fire by the reception desk. I use the term *reception desk* loosely. It was a tall rectangular table with a thick green cloth covering its top. The cost of installing a heating system in the building was not an option. It was almost 1.00 pm. I had occupied myself quite successfully but yearned for someone - anyone - to visit and browse. Better still, I wanted someone to buy something to justify my exorbitant salary, but it was not to be. Andy was not due back until around 4.00 pm and Rob would not be in the whole week. I was alone. Unable to resist temptation, I wandered down to the cellar once more.

CHAPTER NINE - THE CELLAR

As I descended the steps, the smell grew stronger. I had forgotten to take the torch, so I doubled back to retrieve it. I shone the light on the bookcase where I had previously found what I thought were *first editions.* A quick thumb through a few titles confirmed my belief. Some were quite valuable, but they were deteriorating fast. They would already be difficult to sell at a premium. Again, I wondered why they had been left in the cellar?

A noise startled me. I turned to identify its source and fell onto the bookcase. It toppled over, hitting the wall with some force. The torch fell from my hands and ended up the other side of the room. I was disorientated. I had hit my elbow and forehead. The books were strewn around me. I collected myself together before moving toward the torch. A rat scurried into a corner of the room and disappeared. I shone a light on the damage I had caused and saw that the bookcase had disintegrated and there was a sizeable hole in the wall. I picked up the books and placed them at the side of the room. The bookcase was beyond repair. I gathered up the remains of its carcass and stacked it near the books. Upon closer inspection, there appeared to be a void behind the hole, a narrow tunnel.

Noticing blood on my hands, I went back upstairs to the shop to inspect further.

A full-length mirror at the entrance of the shop revealed a cut on my elbow, a graze to my forehead, blood on my cheek, and an embarrassed look on my face. I had been concerned what Andy and Rob might say if I mentioned the first editions in the cellar and had decided not to raise the subject. Now, I was faced with telling them about the demolition job I had undertaken, and this time, there would be no avoiding the admission.

My mobile 'phone reverberated in my pocket. It was a text from Andy. He was unable to get back and asked me to close the shop at the end of the day. *What a relief,* I thought. This would give me time to tidy up and think of a plausible excuse for my antics. Having washed up, I returned to the cellar. The pungent smell hit my nostrils. It was silent, other than a faint sound of the cathedral bells peeling far in the distance. There was a cold feeling as air escaped from the hole into the cellar. I shone the torch beam into the void. I could see about ten feet ahead before there was a turn to the left. It had to be an ancient path or tunnel leading out of the building that had been sealed up at the time the wall was built, perhaps more than five hundred years before. Having caused the hole and discovered what was behind it, curiosity encouraged me to explore further. Andy and Rob's displeasure would not be measured by the size of the hole, but by the fact that a hole existed in the first place.

I picked away at the wattle and daub and quickly created a much bigger hole - far larger than I had originally planned, but it allowed me to squeeze through to the other side on my hands and knees. The torch light guided me. It was clear this void or tunnel was not a natural phenomenon, but man-made. I had moved forward about 10 feet before reaching the turning. I struggled to maneuver and could not see if it went any further. The light eventually revealed a long carefully carved space, which I felt had to have been dug out for a reason. Before I could explore further though, I noticed that the light was beginning to fade. It was time to return to the shop. By the time I presented myself to the mirror for the second time, my eye was showing signs of bruising. I was also covered head to toe in dust.

It was gone 5.00 pm. It was time to lock up and return to the flat to tell Peter what I had discovered. The rain pelted down. My raincoat covered my disheveled clothes, not that anyone would notice. It reminded me of my search for Peter in the woods near the railway station, after the shooting. I was keen to tell him what I had been up to. At the same time, I wondered what kind of mood he would be in. Had my comments about his mood swings yesterday evening done the trick, or would he have reverted to the introspection I had endured the past few months?

Peter was in. He greeted me as I walked through the door. He was in fine form. He had been out walking in the rain most of the day - to clear my mind", he said. It had seemed to work. I let him tell me about his excursion before I told him about the tunnel. I explained in fine detail what had led to its discovery, and he laughed. It was good to see him in a jovial mood, something that had been so lacking recently. He was just as intrigued as me and insisted that we had supper before returning to the bookshop to investigate further. I was hesitant at first; after all, I had been entrusted with the keys, but not so I could abuse them in this way. That said, the thought of exploring the tunnel before morning was tempting, especially when I knew I would need to explain to Andy what I had been up to.

CHAPTER TEN - THE TUNNEL

A rmed with several torches, we crept into the shop. It was eerie, just after 8.40 pm. Peter had never set foot inside before and he looked around, uncertain. I thought it unwise to put the lights on for fear of attracting attention. We were just to use the torches.

Peter commented on the musty smell. "How can you work here? There is such an unpleasant smell about the place." I tried to explain that the smell was a part of the building's charm. After all, it was a 15th century building without any heating, and buildings of this age did smell. We went down to the cellar.

As we descended, I felt the noticeable chill in the air. We shone our torches, quickly revealing the destruction before us. Peter peered through the void and gave his opinion that it was a man-made tunnel.

The Dissolution of the Monasteries during the 16th century had sent the religious community into a frenzy. In most cathedral cities such as Winchester, tunnels were built leading to and from the cathedral for monks and other religious leaders escaping certain death from the King's men. Could it be that I had stumbled across one of those hidden tunnels? I made it clear to Peter that if we investigated further, I did not want to create any additional damage to the property or adversely disturb any history it may reveal. This could prove to be an important find, and if it were, it would need to be reported. There was only room for one at a time, so I would go first. I would get as far as I could, then return so that Peter could take my place and see the tunnel for himself. I crawled on my hands and knees to the first bend about 10 feet from the hole. The beam of light shone ahead as I gradually pushed on until the tunnel increased in width and height. I was now able to sit on my haunches. I provided Peter with a running commentary as I moved. The air further inside was surprisingly fresh. I could hear the faint rumble of traffic above me. I assumed I was beneath the one-way system that ran through the city. As the crow flew, or in this case, the rats ran, I was probably situated about 300 feet from the high street, and a further 900 feet from the cathedral itself - assuming that was the direction the tunnel was travelling.

My back was aching like hell and I had to return to the cellar to stretch out. It was impossible to turn around in such a confined space, so shuffling backwards was the only option. I shouted to Peter I was on my way. Whether he had heard or not, I was not sure. It had taken forty minutes to complete the journey there and back, and when I emerged, Peter was excited to investigate for himself. I stood and stretched out again. It felt good to be upright. Peter went through the hole on his hands and knees in double quick time. I asked him to call out occasionally to let me know he was okay. He made good progress to the bend and inched his way out of sight. His voice became more distant, then it tailed off altogether. I repeatedly called out to him, but no response came. After quite some time I became concerned.

Should I stay where I was and wait to hear from him, or enter the tunnel to see how far he had travelled? I waited a few more minutes and called again, but there was no reply. I had no choice, I had to put myself through the pain of crawling on my hands and knees once more. As far as I could see, neither Peter nor the light from his torch were visible. I called him every few minutes in the hope of hearing his voice. I was nearing the furthest point I had travelled on the first expedition but still there was no sign of him. I was finding breathing difficult. My back complained bitterly, and I had to turn over and lie flat for a few minutes to gain some respite. It was heaven. The absurdity of the situation was not lost on me. I was lying flat on my back in complete darkness, it was cold, and the tunnel was barely supported. It could, in theory, collapse at any moment, burying me alive. Peter had also disappeared, yet there I was, describing my position as *heaven*. Having returned to a kneeling position, I shone my torch. The tunnel meandered left for thirty or so feet, then right. Peter was lighter, slimmer, and younger than me, so I expected him to be in better shape. I called again but still I heard nothing. I was anxious for him, but I had reached as far as I could go, knowing I had the return journey to make. That *heaven* was rapidly turning to hell. Then, a flicker of light in the distance caught my attention. I had to continue. My torch light picked up an image partly propped up against the side wall. It was Peter.

I moved as quickly as I possibly could to get to him, but upon arrival, I found him unconscious. I spoke to him and tried to move him in the limited space available, but there was no response. Concerned, I located a pulse and discerned that he was breathing. Adrenaline rushed through my veins and I felt sick. It had become harder to breath. I had to return to the shop to get help.

I knew it would take considerable time shuffling backward to complete the return journey and during that time, anything could happen to Peter. I turned my neck as best I could and looked backwards. The torch light suggested there had been no movement, so I switched it off and darkness descended. At times like this, the mind operates in overdrive. I found myself questioning everything. Why had I thought it appropriate to go down to the cellar in the first place? Why, having knocked the bookcase over and created the hole, did I think it appropriate to investigate the tunnel rather than reporting it to Andy, as any intelligent adult would do? Why involve Peter in this charade that may cost him his life, a life I had been trying to protect? I felt a sense of self-loathing as I squeezed my way through the hole and back into the cellar. I stood up too quickly and the room began to spin. Bright lights flashed in my head. I collapsed to the floor.

It was pitch black when I came to. I had no idea where I was at first. As I struggled to my feet, it all came back to me. I felt physically sick and had chest pains. I ferreted around in my pocket for the torch and found my watch. It was 11.37 pm. I had been unconscious for some time. I shone the torch through the hole in the wall and shouted to Peter at the top of my voice. Luckily, I heard movement he was slowly clawing his way toward me. He said nothing. He was twenty- five feet away. I could only wait.

I pulled him through the hole, and he slumped to the floor, breathing heavily. He was shaking with cold and barely conscious. His face was pallid, and he was unable to talk. My sense of relief that he was alive was palpable. I had feared the worst. I needed to get help but nothing about this experience or Peter's plight was rational. I sat next to him as he lay there in a semi-conscious state. I started talking about the tunnel and what we should do next. I was high on adrenaline and not thinking clearly. I came to my senses as Peter began to recover and started to talk. He needed medical help and I knew I should call for an ambulance, but I chose not to.

Peter was on the run. Despite the passing of time since the shooting, he was still a *wanted man.* If I called for an ambulance. his identity would be revealed, and he would be arrested. There were bottles of water in the shop. I fetched a couple and encouraged him to drink. He had suffered no injuries as far as I could see; his condition was almost certainly due to exhaustion. We spoke briefly about the ordeal. I asked if I should call for an ambulance, but he was quick to decline the offer. He knew, as I did, what that would lead to. Shortly after midnight, I locked the front door of the shop and we staggered toward the high street like drunks after a night out on the town. We reached the flat and collapsed into our beds.

I had been due to start work the following morning at 9.00 am but it was nearly 1.00 pm when I woke. I was fully dressed and covered in dust. There was a text message on my 'phone from Andy. He would not be in today. With a sense of relief, I dropped back onto the pillow and slept.

I heard Peter calling out incoherently in his sleep. He was having nightmares. I checked on him several times but chose not to wake him. It was early evening before he appeared in the sitting room. I had showered and dressed some hours earlier before settling down to think about recent events. He seemed fragile and in a mild state of confusion. I wanted to discover what had happened to him in the tunnel, but this was not the time to broach the subject. I would let him tell me when he was ready. I was to discover that as a child, he had suffered from vertigo. Panic attacks were a regular occurrence until his late teens. He explained that having reached the point where I found him, the torch light had gone out, leaving him in darkness. He had had a panic attack and found it difficult to breath. Confined, he knew there was no quick escape. He shouted to me but had no voice. He remembered feeling a cold chill run through him and described in detail what he saw next.

The tunnel suddenly lit up, as it would on the set of a movie, and fog came toward him on a breeze. Out of the haze and in the distance, he saw monks on their hands and knees coming toward him, screaming, fighting to escape the tunnel. The nearer they came, the louder the screams. Their faces were disfigured, their eyes had been removed, and blood was everywhere. Then, when they were only feet away, he passed out.

By the expression on his face and the way he described the event, it had been a harrowing experience. Of course, the panic attack and his shortness of breath had led to him hallucinating, but there was no equivocation as far as he was concerned - it was real. It happened. As he told his story, I listened intently, avoiding questions. He was tired and when he had finished giving me his account, he returned to bed. He spoke little about the experience over the next few days and continued to have nightmares. He also became withdrawn once more.

It was late. Andy would almost certainly be back in the bookshop the next morning and I was still wrestling with the dilemma of what to tell him. It was not a conversation I relished. I know I had no right to enter the cellar in the first place, let alone destroy a bookcase and put a large hole in the wall. Worse still, how could I justify returning to the tunnel with Peter to investigate? To add to my foolishness, I had then allowed Peter to become trapped, risking his life.

Sleep was intermittent. I thrashed about for most of the night. Eventually, I got up early and meandered around the flat. I was still undecided whether to tell Andy the unadulterated truth or to fabricate a story that would at least sound plausible. I skipped breakfast and went to the bookshop to prepare for the encounter.

Andy arrived a few minutes after me. We exchanged the usual pleasantries; there was plenty of opportunity for me to spill the beans and offer an apology, but I failed to find the right words. I decided the truth was not an option and I needed to think on my feet. I felt like a naughty schoolboy outside the headmaster's office, waiting to be punished for some wrongdoing. At that moment, Andy turned to me and said, "Oh, by the way, there are some first editions in the cellar I've been meaning to bring up to the shop for ages. Can you get them for me? Get the torch - the lights are out down there." I responded to his command with a nod. This was the opportunity to put things right.

Dutifully, I took the torch and went down to retrieve the books. "What condition are they in?" he called down to me. "They seem okay", I replied. "A bit dusty. Looks messy down here and there is a large hole in the wall. What happened?" I climbed the stairs back to Andy.

How I had the audacity to say what I did surprised even me, but it was the first thing that came into my head. I was thinking on my feet. Andy sounded confused. "Hole? I had better investigate. Come with me." The battery in the torch was low from the night before, but there was still enough light to expose the bookcase and the hole. "Bloody hell! What on earth happened here?" he exclaimed. I remained silent. "Would you go upstairs and bring some AA batteries down? These are fading." I returned with a new set and Andy switched on the torch, shining a light beyond the hole. "This looks like a tunnel of some description. How on earth did the bookcase end up in pieces on the floor?"

Feeling distinctly uncomfortable, I mumbled the first words that came into my head that contributed nothing at all to Andy's enquiry. I was working on the premise that his question was rhetorical, and he was not expecting me to have any credible answers although I was all-knowledgeable. If he had looked at my face, he would have seen my guilt writ large. The headmaster wanted answers, the truth. I could only nod silently and shrug my shoulders.

"I'll need to speak to Rob about this. I guess he'll know what happened and has forgotten to tell me." He peered into the tunnel again and handed me the torch, asking me if I would like to take a closer look. I peered into the void, knowing what I would see. The drama of the previous evening played over in my mind. I handed the torch back and mustered a few words of surprise. We returned to the shop. Andy 'phoned Rob and to his surprise, he knew nothing about the hole in the wall.

During the following months, archeologists and officials from the city council visited the shop and the tunnel was excavated. It was confirmed to be a 16th century medieval passage that led from the basement of the bookshop to the inner sanctum of the cathedral, to provide safe refuge for fleeing clergy and supporters of the faith. It was considered a significant find and the size and sophistication of the passage suggested a volume of people would have used it, some of whom probably lived for days in wider parts of the construction before fleeing. Several artifacts were discovered from the period including sackcloth, animal bones - suggesting people prepared food there - ornaments, and skeletal remains. Far more importantly, I thought, was the discovery of a Roman burial beneath a section of the tunnel that lay just inside the cathedral grounds. The burial was in an excellent state of preservation and accompanied by a hoard of gold coins in mint condition, extremely rare jewels, two pristine swords, and other items from the period that were considered priceless. My discovery of the tunnel had led to the bookshop becoming a shrine for those with an interest in Winchester history.

The subsequent PR value and attention the bookshop enjoyed attracted a flow of new customers and much needed revenue enabling Andy and Rob to devote their time fully to the business. In addition to selling books, they started offering visits to the cellar. Tourists from all over the world visited Winchester every year, now they had another attraction to see. Myths circulated about the mysterious passage being haunted by monks who had broken down the wall attempting to escape the king's men. Oddly enough, in flicking through a book of Winchester history during an idle moment I came across text that perfectly described the scene Peter had portrayed after he emerged from the tunnel *of monks on their hands and knees coming toward him, screaming, fighting to escape*. I had no idea what to make of it.

To this day, *the hole in the wall* and the discovery of a secret passage remain a mystery. Why had the bookcase fallen to pieces revealing the hole? Why was there a hole in the wall in the first place? Perhaps the vision that Peter saw that evening in the tunnel was true after all? The penalty for my curiosity and resulting dishonesty that had risked Peter's life in the process, was that the secret of the *hole in the wall* would have to remain just that - a secret.

CHAPTER ELEVEN - A CHRISTMAS I WILL NEVER FORGET

The bookshop was busy most days and I was pleased for Andy and Rob, but I felt a fraud. I found it increasingly difficult to withhold the truth and thought it right that I quit my job. Andy and Rob were disappointed when I told them of my plan to leave and begged me to stay. Business was brisk and visits to the cellar were very much a part of the daily routine, but I knew what I was doing was right.

It was approaching Christmas. Winchester hosted a wonderful Christmas market and people would travel far and wide to visit. Families spent the day meandering around the stalls and the cathedral and there was a sense of excitement in the air. But for Peter, and to a lesser extent, me, it was anything but a joyous time. His mood swings see-sawed as he continued to pine for Mary, and I suffered as a result.

I kept in touch with Mandy, who was still running the business in London and all was well, but she was understandably concerned that I remained away and asked again if I was planning to return.

Having left the bookshop's employ, I dreaded spending the festive season locked away in the flat with Peter. Since his trauma in the tunnel, and despite my encouragement, he had made no effort to drag himself out of his depressed mental state. He would only speak to me when he had to, and he rarely ventured out.

It was a spur of the moment decision, but I decided to pay a surprise visit to Eleanor, a childhood friend, and her husband Mike, on Christmas day. They lived about twenty-five miles from Winchester, in a village called Odiham. Eleanor had a twin sister, Caroline and an older brother, David, who were born in Africa. I had had a brief affair with Eleanor prior to her marriage to Mike, which had caused a rift between the sisters. Mike never knew of the affair and Eleanor was keen to ensure he never found out. I felt terribly guilty at the time. The two sisters were incredibly close, as twins often are, and my intervention had undermined that bond. Caroline was jealous of me and accused me of driving a wedge between them. She was vindictive and vowed never to speak to Eleanor again. On several occasions, she threatened to tell Mike about the affair; whether she ever did or not, I did not know. I hoped for the latter, otherwise my visit might prove to be more than a little awkward. All the same, though, I was prepared to take the risk.

It was selfish but I decided not to tell Peter of my plans until Christmas Eve. The last thing I wanted was an inquisition. The day finally arrived, and Peter was watching television. Up to this point, he had not mentioned Christmas once. Immediately after supper, I announced that I was leaving to visit relatives in Odiham in the morning. If I had been expecting a reaction, any reaction, I was to be disappointed. He said nothing; he just nodded and went off to his bedroom.

I had planned to get up early. My plan was to cycle to Odiham on a bike I had bought from a second hand shop a few days earlier. It was stored in the bin cupboard. I had remembered Eleanor's address but had not communicated with her for at least fifteen or so years. There was a strong possibility that she and Mike would no longer be living there, but that was a chance I was prepared to take. Christmas morning was cold and windy, but the rain held off and the sun was attempting to break through. I got up as planned and quietly moved about the flat to avoid waking Peter. I was hoping that by the time I returned, he would be in a better frame of mind. Upon exiting the flat, I left a Christmas card for him on the doormat.

My bike had ten gears and my immediate challenge was finding them. The streets were deserted. I felt positive and enthusiastic about my adventure. I was not fit, and I knew it. My calf and thigh muscles served me with confirmation as I ascended the first hill. I was dressed inappropriately for a bike ride. I wore smart black trousers, at least the smartest ones I had in the wardrobe. They had originally been part of a suit that someone had donated to the charity shop. I also wore a long-sleeve check shirt with a slight tear in the collar, and a bright red ski jacket I was confident had never seen the slopes before. On my feet was a pair of well-worn trainers. I had no hat or gloves to wear and was soon to regret that omission. I was very conscious that my appearance for a Christmas morning surprise visit was not all it could have been, but it was the best I could muster.

Not long into the journey the exertion was taking its toll. I was breathing deeply. Saddle discomfort, to put it mildly, is the curse of amateur cyclists and I was suffering. My head and hands were freezing but despite all that, I was pleased I had decided to undertake the journey and looked forward to the prospect of meeting up with Eleanor and Mike again, albeit with some trepidation. It was late morning when I arrived in Odiham. It had proved to be more arduous a journey than I had imagined. 25 miles on a heavy bike that benefitted from only occasional gear changes was not easy. As I reached the town the church bells rang out and people were milling about. I got off the bike inelegantly, and with much relief, was able to stop a passerby to get directions. Rectory Gardens was just two minutes away, in the direction of the bells.

Rather than mount the bike again, I chose to walk. I pushed the bike slowly down Odiham High Street. Sure enough, Rectory Gardens was opposite the church and number one was the first property in sight. It was a large, thatched house, probably dating from the mid sixteenth century. I stopped outside and paused for a moment to take in its charm. A black Labrador bounded from a side gate and headed straight for me as though I was expected. It barked and wagged its tail the way they do, and I felt instantly welcome. What would I say? Why was I visiting? Where had I been for the past umpteen years? Was I right to be calling now, on Christmas Day, when family were almost certainly gathering? I was distracted by the dog's affection when a door shut suddenly at the side of the house and a woman came walking down the path in my direction. At that moment, the dog lunged at me and knocked me and the bike over. As I struggled to my feet, I heard a familiar voice. "Barney! Barney! I'm so sorry – you'd think you were the first person he'd seen in years!" "It has been a few years, I'll admit," I replied instinctively. The woman looked at me quizzically at first, then her eyes lit up and she rushed towards me and hugged me. "What on earth are you doing here? This can't be a coincidence!"

Eleanor was pleasantly surprised to see me and now, somewhat lost for words. She looked beautiful, just as I remembered her. She was tall, with flowing brown hair, piercing blue eyes, and a complexion that was almost translucent. She wore a long, jet-black coat with a rust brown fur collar that fitted tightly around her neck, it looked as though she was about to go to church. My own appearance was somewhat less appealing. My trousers were tucked into my socks and mud ran up my leg. "I can't believe it. Is it really you, Lawrence"? We threw our arms around each other with great affection and remained locked together for what seemed like an age. It was a wonderful feeling.

As I previously recounted, as children, we had had a strong bond and a natural affection for each other, and when we were old enough to appreciate our physical differences, we became close. Absurd as it seems now, we had talked of spending the rest of our lives together. But then, she met Mike and fell in love and I was consigned to a brief affair one weekend before their marriage. We both felt extremely guilty that it had happened but happen it did. Those feelings of long ago were now rekindled in an instant. I wondered if Mike would be as pleased to see me. Having prized ourselves apart but not persuaded Barney that I should be left alone, we walked back to the house and entered.

The temperature immediately struck me. Although my heart had been warmed by seeing Eleanor, my bones were cold and needed to thaw. The house was surprisingly quiet apart from the sound of voices from a radio in another room. There were no obvious decorations acknowledging the fact that it was Christmas, nor was there the smell of roast turkey in the oven as we entered the hallway. Huge oak timber beams supported the ceiling. There was a beautifully carved spiral staircase leading to the first floor. To the left an old, solid oak door that led to the drawing room. We entered to a log fire that was roaring, demanding my company.

We stood by the fire, exchanging what were the obvious questions of two people that had not met for some years. I learned a lot in a short time. Tragically, Mike and their daughter, Charlotte, had drowned in a yachting accident some years earlier. She had never re-married. Understandably, it was an awkward conversation to have so soon after arriving. There was a solid knock on the front door. Eleanor broke away to answer it. What had escaped her mind since I had turned up unannounced on her doorstep, was a Christmas lunch date with friends in the village. Jack Forrester, a local farmer, and his wife, Lucy, had invited her to join them for lunch. Eleanor had planned to take the dog for a walk before setting off, but then I arrived. Jack was on his way to church and had knocked to say hello. Acutely aware that my arrival had thrown a spanner in the works, I suggested that I leave and return another day. Fortunately for me, though, my protestations were outvoted, and I was invited to accompany Eleanor to lunch. She stood there like the Beauty and me, the Beast. My trousers were firmly held in place by my socks and Barney was still finding my presence exciting. He tugged at the laces in my battered trainers, laying a strong claim to them. I was the first to acknowledge that their condition warranted new ownership and so, he acquired them.

It was fortunate for me that Eleanor had kept the contents of Mike's wardrobe - not, she insisted, because of a sense of loyalty or over-indulgent mourning, but simply because she had never got round to sorting them out. As my present attire was somewhat inappropriate for Christmas lunch and I now had no trainers, she insisted I helped myself to whatever fitted. We climbed the stairs and entered the master bedroom, complete with huge walk-in dressing room. On the left was a twelve-foot run of wardrobes which, as I discovered, was crammed with the most remarkable collection of men's clothes. On the right, another similar run housed Eleanor's collection. By chance, Mike and I were almost the same size. Eleanor excused herself and invited me to try on the clothes. Jackets, trousers, and shirts all fitted perfectly and felt wonderful to the touch. There were dozens of Italian silk ties and too many pairs of leather shoes for me to count. I remembered Mike as a dapper chap. I, too, had held a passion for wearing quality clothes from Jermyn Street, but that was long gone.

I wondered what had happened to my more modest wardrobe at home in Knightsbridge. In fact, I wondered if I still had a home at all.

I called Eleanor to pass judgement on my choice of attire. I had chosen a white shirt with cut-away collar, navy blue suit, blue patterned tie, and a pair of Oxford brogues. She looked at me fondly and her eyes welled up. I could see she had mixed emotions seeing Mike's clothes worn again. She hesitated to pass judgment, then raised a broad smile of approval. I had been in her company for less than an hour. During that time, I had been warmly greeted, introduced to the local farmer, invited to Christmas lunch, and I was now standing there, dressed like a lord. I could not remember the last time I felt so good.

After a hot bath, I went down to the drawing room and we had coffee. Barney, deprived of his walk and now bored with me and my trainers, wanted exercise. Eleanor insisted that I stay by the fire whilst she took him out. She was gone almost half an hour.

My intention was not to pry in any way, but I was fascinated to look at the photographs on top of the piano in the drawing room. There were several of Mike on his yacht and the three of them together. Charlotte was beautiful, just like her mother. When Eleanor returned, Barney greeted me like a long-lost friend and took an immediate liking to my - or should I say, Mike's - shoes. This time, though, I was not about to give them up. Eleanor took him into another room and returned. I was pleased to be in her company. The torch I had held for her had not diminished, let alone extinguished. I was reasonably confident she was pleased to see me too. An hour passed and it was time to head off to Jack's for lunch. I was hungry, but truth be known, I would have preferred staying put. We had settled into the comfort of each other's company and I did not want to break the spell. Running late, we left the house and made our way to the farmhouse in Eleanor's Porsche. I was high on adrenaline and low on confidence. I wondered how well I would juggle the truth and fabrication of my life at the party to protect my current circumstances, and at the same time, not lose Eleanor's affection.

When we arrived, we wended our way toward the farmhouse as the sounds of conversation and laughter intensified. The journey was short. Jack greeted us at the door with champagne and a broad smile. He seemed genuinely happy that Eleanor and I were together. There was a throng of activity awaiting us. It was Christmas, after all, and it felt good.

It had been some years since I had experienced such a feeling of contentment. *How soon the memory fades,* I thought. How easy it is to forget how to enjoy the company of others. For a moment, I thought about Peter, alone in the flat, and the miserable Christmas he must be having. I felt guilty, but that feeling soon evaporated as I consumed several glasses of champagne.

By the time we were summoned for lunch, I felt quite drunk. I had chatted incessantly since the moment we arrived. I had not seen or spoken to Eleanor at all. *Such nice people,* I thought. *I could get to like this lifestyle again.*

Over lunch, I sat opposite Eleanor. Everyone around me, especially the women, were desperate to know all about me and how we got to know each other. It was apparent how much she was liked. More than that, she was admired by her friends and that was easy to understand. She had a natural, spontaneous personality and a genuine interest in others. Despite chatting with those either side of me, my attention was really fixed on her. I watched her every movement, her every expression. Her laughter was infectious. She was a beautiful woman, with sparkling eyes and a wonderful smile. When our eyes met, her facial expression implied that she was happy to have me at the party. I wondered what signals I was giving off. Was I too intense? It had been a long time since I had felt this way about anyone, and I did not want to make a fool of myself.

Lunch was a complete indulgence. Eventually, we all stumbled our way through to an enormous sitting room. Few were sober and spirits were high. The intimacy and camaraderie of friendship was evident. Over lunch, most of my conversational time had been spent with Lucy. She was Jack's partner, and one of Eleanor's closest friends. The moment I entered the sitting room, she made a beeline for me and there was no escaping her. She was an articulate, intelligent woman and had a wonderful sense of fun. She gently shoved me onto a two-seater sofa and planted herself next to me, demanding to know my life story. If only I could tell her. I was at a loss for what to say. Eleanor had mentioned in the car that Lucy was a county court judge, which accounted for her forthright questioning.

Fabricating stories was not my forte. My experience with the bookshop saga was evidence of that, but that was precisely what I had to do if I were to survive this lunch party with any credibility. So far, I had managed to avoid telling Eleanor much, and was certainly not prepared for the kind of interrogation that Judge Lucy clearly had in mind. Fearful I would blurt something out about Peter and the shooting, I took a measured approach to my responses. I did so much want to tell the truth, but I knew that sometimes - and this was one of those times - the truth could do nothing but harm.

For almost ten minutes, I ducked and dived, trying to manipulate the conversation around to her, but she was having none of it. With alcohol loosening my tongue, she prodded and probed until I had no idea what I was saying. Thankfully, she got up after a while and left me to join another conversation.

Eleanor spotted me on my own and came over. She dropped down beside me and kissed me gently on the cheek. What a wonderful feeling. She briefed me on local gossip and people at the party. Apparently, everyone wanted to know who I was. Were we a couple? She was loving the attention and intrigue. I wished I felt the same way. She turned to me and said how happy she was that I had turned up unannounced on her doorstep. The look in her eyes confirmed the sincerity of her words. We had only been re-united for a few hours and I knew I was in love with her.

CHAPTER TWELVE - THE

HORROR OF LOSING HER

W
e left the party late and Eleanor insisted I stay the night. Our host was nowhere to be seen. He had consumed more alcohol than the two of us put together, so a lift back to Eleanor's house was out of the question. We rang for a taxi, which arrived quite quickly and left the Porsche in the driveway. It was bitterly cold. The fresh air rushed to my head and I knew I was in for a terrible hangover in the morning.

Our laughter and childlike conduct failed to amuse the taxi driver. Why would it? He had probably been deprived of a wonderful day at home with his family. The compensation was a double fare which, under the circumstances, seemed less than generous. After all, it was Christmas day. Embarrassingly, I had no money so Eleanor settled the bill upon arrival. We crawled out of the car and staggered to the front door. I could hear the dog barking.

The warmth of the house felt good. Eleanor went to the kitchen. I could hear her talking to Barney as she let him out. It had been a wonderful day. It could not have been better. My instinct was to put my arms around her, squeeze hard, and not let go, but caution seemed the better option. I was confident that she had enjoyed my company at the party, but I did not want to seem forward. I decided to let her make the first move. She busied herself for what seemed like an age before acknowledging I was there. Then, she turned to face me with two cups of coffee, put them down, and threw her arms around me. We embraced. As she drew back slowly, I stared into her crystal-clear eyes that would melt any man's heart. We hugged again. It felt good. We picked up the coffee and made our way to the sitting room.

We were both dead beat but that did not stop us reminiscing about the party. She wanted to know who I had spoken to, what was said, and what I thought of her friends. I struggled with the finer details, conscious that I had lied to Lucy about my past. I could barely remember what I said. I felt wretched. Eleanor's friends were desperate to know more about me. She had told them about our childhood days of infatuation and about me turning up at her garden gate that morning.

Earlier in the day, I had let slip that I was knowledgeable about art and antiques. I had mentioned I had a business in London. So, it was no surprise that she asked me to look at some of the antiques in the room. She wanted to know if she had bought wisely. I was tired and to be honest, I did not want the distraction, but I obliged and spent twenty minutes appraising various pieces. Excitedly, she left the room and returned with two beautifully carved boxes. One contained some of Mike's possessions, including at least eight rare, high quality vintage gold watches and other items of great value. The other box contained her jewels. "So, what do you think? Was Mike a generous husband?" We were both suffering from the alcohol consumed at the party and I was tired, but she was as high as a kite and insisted I look at them. I was impressed by both collections. How could I not have been? Diamonds and watches were not my specialism, but I knew enough to say that there were many tens of thousands of pounds of value in Mike's box alone.

She went to the kitchen and came back with a large plastic supermarket bag, put both boxes inside, and asked me to take them away in the morning to get a valuation for insurance. The fact that it was Boxing Day, and that I had arrived at the house earlier in the day on a bicycle, had escaped her mind. But it was pointless mentioning such trivia now. She was insistent that I take the bag into the hallway and place it near the door; I was not to forget it. Reluctantly, I did as I was asked. It seemed a little risky leaving them where an intruder could easily find them, but again, I stayed silent. It was a surreal experience stimulated by alcohol and not quite the way I wanted to end the evening.

I vaguely remember Eleanor making another coffee but thereafter, my mind went blank, at least until I woke the next morning at around 9.20 am. I was lying naked in Eleanor's bed and she was asleep next to me. I was startled and confused. Why was I in Eleanor's bed? Did anything happen between us? My head was spinning from the predicted hangover. My mood had changed completely.

The joy and excitement of the previous day deserted me. Instead, I felt an odd personal loathing. I desperately wanted Eleanor's affections but not this way, and not in a drunken stupor. I feared she would feel the same loathing when she awoke. I lay there, wondering what to do and what to say. Almost ten minutes passed, and she had not moved an inch. She was perfectly still and surprisingly cold to the touch. I grew anxious and gradually moved my body away from hers to look at her face. I was instinctively checking for signs of life. It is an expression often used without thinking about its true meaning, but on this occasion, there was no escape, there were no signs of life, Eleanor was dead.

I leapt out of the bed. The rush of blood to my head made my heart race and I could feel myself losing balance. I looked back at her. Gingerly, I went to her side of the bed and looked at her more closely. I brushed the back of my hand against her ashen cheek and searched for a pulse. She was cold. She must have been dead for some time. Overwhelmed, I began to sob uncontrollably. The duvet completely covered her torso, leaving only her head visible. I peeled it back from her body to see if there were any obvious signs of death. She lay on her side and was wearing a nightdress. There was no evidence of blood or an attack of any kind. I wondered if I had somehow accidentally smothered her in the night. I pulled the duvet over her body leaving her head exposed. I could not accept the fact that she was gone, and I felt that pulling the duvet completely over her would leave me in no doubt. Then, I put on one of Mike's dressing gowns and left the room. Descending the stairs, I was greeted by Barney. He was excited to see me and barked continuously, the sound reverberating in my head. He followed me to the kitchen, demanding breakfast. I closed the kitchen door and hunted around for dog food. For a few minutes, I was distracted and in an odd way, I completely forgot about Eleanor. Perhaps that is how the mind deals with such trauma. It did not last long. With Barney fed, I sat down and began to shake. I continued to feel sick. Was it the level of alcohol in my bloodstream or the shock of finding her? Either way, it was irrelevant. She was dead and I had to decide what to do next.

Ten minutes passed in a flash and I woke from a trance to find myself staring at the tablecloth. I could see Barney in front of me, barking, but I was deaf. I wondered where my mind had been. My legs quivered as I got up. Barney immediately demanded to be let out and I obliged, closing the back door behind him. I turned to face the kitchen door and collapsed.

I was having a panic attack, just as Peter had in the tunnel. Breathing became extremely difficult and I had no option but to stay on the floor. I thought I was about to die. I felt tortured, both mentally and physically. It took some minutes before the panic passed and I was able to compose myself. I could not believe what was happening. Was it all a bad dream?

My instinct was to 'phone for an ambulance and the police, but for some inexplicable reason I just could not do it - at least, not yet. I wanted to go back to the bedroom in the desperate hope that it was a bad dream, and she would be asleep or dressing. I thought of making her a cup of tea, but the absurdity struck me. Knowing that there was almost no hope of her being alive, I slowly ascended the stairs, keeping my eyes focused on the bedroom door. It was slightly ajar. The moment of truth. I gently pushed the door open and looked across to the bed. There had been no movement. The duvet remained where I had left it. Her head was motionless. She was dead. She was dead! I shrieked out loud. I turned, closed the door, and returned to the kitchen.

I reflected on the short time we had spent together at the party, and afterwards, when we had returned. I was in love with her but now it was over before we really got to know each other again. I was incapable of thinking clearly. I was not fearful for my own situation; as far as I knew, I was not to blame for her death and an inquest would discover the truth. However, I knew that my plight could very well affect Peter's freedom. He was still on the run, and if I became embroiled in Eleanor's death, it may well expose him in some way. I became increasingly aware of Barney howling outside, wondering why he had not been let in. I opened the door and he raced passed me. The excitement he was experiencing was matched only by my despair. I sat down at the kitchen table and he returned to me, burying his head in my lap.

I considered my options. I could pack up my modest possessions and simply cycle away, just as I had arrived. Of course, that was absurd. Sooner or later, Eleanor would be discovered dead and I would be the focus of a manhunt. And anyway, aside from the ludicrousness of the idea, I could not do such a thing. I was in love with her. I could 'phone Jack, but what would that achieve? He knew nothing of me. Everything led back to the obvious. I had to call the police and deal with situation as best I could. As I hesitated to pick up the 'phone, the doorbell rang, which made me jump. Thinking quickly, I decided not to open it. Barney started to bark. It rang again. It was Lucy. She looked through the window and saw me standing in the hallway in Mike's dressing gown. I had to open the door. Barney rushed forward, excited at seeing her.

"Hello Lawrence, not disturbing you, am I? I was just passing and wanted to make sure you got back okay yesterday evening. Hope you enjoyed the party?" I stood there, unable to move or say anything. "Are you okay? Lawrence, are you okay? Where's Eleanor?" Without hesitating to wait for my answer, she took the initiative and pushed past me. "Eleanor, Eleanor, are you in dear? Just passing and thought I would pop in for a natter." She turned back and faced me. I said nothing. She noticed me shaking and took control immediately, helping me into a chair. "What's going on are you ill or something? Is Eleanor okay?" The awfulness of the situation suddenly hit me, and I started to cry like a baby. Lucy left me and went into the kitchen. Barney followed. She let him out. She went into every room downstairs, looking for Eleanor, then she started to ascend the stairs toward the bedrooms. I shouted out, "She's dead, *dead!*" She looked back at me, startled, but continued toward the bedroom and entered. There was no scream, no manic response from Lucy. She was cool, calm, and collected. She came back down, 'phoned for the police, then returned to the bedroom. Within what seemed like minutes two cars had arrived and three policemen approached the front door. Lucy took charge. I remained in the chair. They went to the bedroom to see the body, then returned to talk to me. Initially, they were courteous and sympathetic. A few minutes later, two more policemen and an ambulance arrived. Within the hour, I had dressed in more of Mike's clothes and was being questioned at the station.

It was a surreal experience. I explained in minute detail who I had met and what had happened since my arrival, and they seemed reasonably satisfied with the answers I gave. At least, I thought they were. But the personal questions about me, where I lived, what I did for a living, and why I was visiting was somehow less believable, and they knew it. Thinking on my feet, which is rarely a good thing, exposed the flaws in my story. The tone of their questioning changed. I was assured the chat we were having was routine and there was no need for legal representation. Why would there be? Soon, though, it became apparent that I was their key suspect. Six hours later, still feeling physically ill and mentally exhausted, I was led to a cell to stew. At that point I had not been formally charged but was being held for further questioning. I still made no effort to secure a lawyer, believing the truth would come out and I would be released.

I was wrong. Soon after, I was arrested for Eleanor's murder.

CHAPTER THIRTEEN - TRIAL

AND IMPRISONMENT

I was held in custody without bail. It took four months to bring the case to trial. It was a living hell. Eleanor had been poisoned with a rare and almost untraceable substance that reacted with saliva and brought about certain death. The evidence showed that the ingested substance had been consumed during the preceding twenty-four hours. By my own admission, I had spent most of that time with her alone - not at the party though, as we were separated most of the afternoon chatting to different people.

I knew I was not the guilty party, so who was? According to the many testimonies at the trial, Eleanor had no enemies. I witnessed her popularity as she swept from one group to another and saw people's faces lighting up with joy upon seeing her. What motive could there possibly be for any one of these people to kill her? My barrister argued that it was not inconceivable that the substance was lying dormant and Eleanor had just happened to touch it and transfer it to her mouth unknowingly. That theory was rejected by the prosecution. It had to be premeditated.

I had no recollection of getting into Eleanor's bed. I had no recollection of what happened after putting the plastic shopping bag containing her and Mike's jewels in the hallway. I knew I had not been in such a drunken state to cause me to black out and wipe my memory clean. There were exhaustive inquiries tracing everyone Eleanor had had contact with during the days leading up to her death, especially those at the party. They were all interviewed, but the finger of the law pointed in my direction. A miniscule amount of the substance that killed Eleanor had apparently been traced to Mike's shirt cuff, the shirt I was wearing, and, as the rest of my story was flawed, I was the obvious suspect. There was another piece of crucial evidence that went against me. The police found the bag of jewels in the hallway with my fingerprints all over them. The prosecuting counsel successfully alleged that I had turned up at Eleanor's house unannounced with the plan to steal her valuables. I was known to her so winning her affection would be easy. I was desperate. I had taken the lethal substance with me as a precaution in case it was necessary to kill her and make a getaway. They were unable to discover how I had obtained the substance or why I had had to use it, but they were certain of one thing: use it I did. It was also put to the jury that the police investigation had taken them to the flat I shared with Peter. A wanted murderer. Perhaps we had planned the robbery together that led to Eleanor's death? Of course, Peter would be as shocked as I was to discover I was being charged for murder.

The trial lasted seven weeks. For most of the time, I sat staring incredulously at the ornamentally carved heraldry above the judge's head. It was as though I were a fly on the wall, in no way participating or otherwise involved in the proceedings. My story was considered so weak I was advised not to take the witness stand. I duly obliged. Due process of law took effect and a jury unanimously found me guilty of murder. I was sentenced to life in HMP Belmarsh where I would serve no fewer than 12 years. I was taken down.

When the verdict was announced and I heard my sentence, I was surprisingly calm. I was mentally exhausted and just wanted it to be over. I had been found guilty of a crime I had not committed. A subsequent appeal was turned down; there was no new evidence. During the trial, and unbeknown to me, there had been a media frenzy about the case and my motives for murdering Eleanor. It was all fantasy. It was an absurd story lacking any credibility, but the jury believed it. Why had I not 'phoned the police to tell them of Eleanor's death? Apparently, it was the unexpected arrival of Lucy that had wrecked my plan to escape. It was her that had called the police.

Finding Peter, a wanted murderer sharing the flat, destroyed any credibility I had. He too was arrested and brought to trial, where he was found guilty of murdering Mary's husband and imprisoned. I had given the police my address, and it had inevitably led them to him. I could have lied. When Jack had visited the house prior to the lunch party and had witnessed the scruffy clothes I wore when I arrived. I could have said I was homeless. *No fixed abode.* Alas, the idea did not enter my head.

I served the full 12 years, during which I often wondered if I was sane. There was a time during the second year of incarceration when I convinced myself that I had in fact murdered Eleanor. I had been found guilty by an independent jury and all the evidence pointed my way. The substance had been found on the shirt I was wearing, and I was the last person to see her alive. I had no recollection of what happened that final evening, so I had to be guilty. Didn't I?

CHAPTER FOURTEEN - A NEW

LIFE ON THE OUTSIDE

I left HMP Belmarsh at precisely 3.00 pm on a Wednesday afternoon. It was a cold, damp day, but it mattered little. I had nothing more than another man's clothes on my back. I had chosen another suit, shirt, tie, and brogues from Mike's wardrobe when I dressed that fateful morning after the police arrived and before they took me to the station for questioning. I looked like a businessman ready for the next deal, but I felt like a fraud. I had lost weight in prison and the clothes fitted badly. There was a musty smell to them. There was no hiding the fact that, like me, they had barely seen the light of day in twelve years.

I had had more than enough time while imprisoned to relive the ecstasy and nightmare of the short time spent with Eleanor, and the intense feelings that had so quickly enveloped me. I also had time to think of all the possible scenarios that might give a plausible explanation of what happened leading up to her death, but my mind was blank. I knew it was the poison that killed her, but the unanswered questions were who was responsible, and why? To my knowledge, the possibility of Eleanor committing suicide was not raised at the trial. At least, I do not recall the subject being discussed, but I thought there had to be a possibility. Was Eleanor depressed and suicidal before I arrived on Christmas morning, and I had lifted her spirits? There were no signs of melancholy at the party - quite the contrary, in fact. Was there an investigation into her mental health with her GP? I had no answers to these questions, and I knew there was little point torturing myself; no one would listen anyway. Perversely, toward the end of my sentence, not only had I convinced myself that I murdered her, but I also wanted to believe I had to stop the mental torment I was inflicting upon myself. I was exhausted with the effort of thinking and regurgitating scenario after scenario, possibility after possibility, but getting nowhere. Looking back now, with a level head, I know I did not kill her.

I was not seeking retribution for being wrongly imprisoned. We all make mistakes, as the jury had in my trial. As human beings, we are fallible and quite capable of listening to a well-articulated argument but still come to the wrong conclusion. The founding principles of our democracy give an independent jury the responsibility to review all the evidence and come to a decision on the fate of the accused, and that is how it should be. The mind can play cruel tricks when there is so much time available for reflection, to the point at which you doubt your own innocence, just as I had. If, and only if sanity prevails, you then return to everyday life and work hard to re-assure your sub-conscious mind that you are not the monster you have been held up to be.

Of course, pleading innocence as so many do in the first few weeks and months of incarceration is a dangerous pastime. Inmates do not take kindly to those seeking a sympathetic ear. It is a sign of weakness. Those that tread that path quickly learn how brutal prison life can be. Violent flare ups are a part of the daily norm. You learn quickly. You adopt a different persona in word and deed if you are to survive. It is extremely hard to describe the mental anguish one endures in such circumstances but endure it you must if you are to remain safe from harm.

During my imprisonment, I had discovered a great deal about human beings, their strengths, weaknesses, frustrations, and motivations. For an avid reader and book lover, the most revealing of my discoveries was the high incidence of dyslexia among the prison population. I could see a clear pathway that had led to their predicament. In simple terms, those with dyslexia find it extremely hard to read and pay attention. Words jumble and jump about on a page, which causes enormous frustration for those affected. It seemed obvious to me that if a child had undiagnosed dyslexia, they would be likely to underperform in class, no matter how bright they were. If you cannot make sense of the words a teacher writes on a white board or read the text in a book, it will engender frustration. Frustration leads to anger and anger to unwanted behaviors. Not being understood or listened to, leads many teenagers into trouble. They will often bully others as a way of working out their frustration. Bullies are vulnerable at heart. They know no other way of expressing themselves than being angry with life, and are often prone to violence, drug taking, and various levels of criminality. They have difficulty building and maintaining relationships. As I said, a high percentage of those who were incarcerated with me were dyslexic. They could not read and write, and the world was different for them. I genuinely believed that if society had done more to identify and treat dyslexia in the young, we would have fewer people incarcerated in our jails.

As the years pass in prison, it can get easier, but you also become hardened to the way of life. It is only in your mind, through your thoughts, that you can be true to yourself. I saw examples of that in a minority of inmates. I anguished over the circumstances of my incarceration and, consequentially, I suffered. Over the millennia, animals have had to evolve to their surroundings. The same is true of man.

I sucked in the fresh air and turned to take one last look at the grey, imposing building that had housed me for the past 12 years. There was no one to say goodbye to, and no one to welcome me into my new life. I was on my own. I was given an allowance and temporary accommodation in Guildford for a month, together with an address to report to if I had difficulties. A job was arranged for me at a wholesale bakery that distributed bread and cakes to shops. I was expected to report for duty the following Monday. After twelve years away from mainstream society, the bakery was a godsend and an opportunity to gain a first footing in my new life, but I was consumed by a fear of the unknown. This was not the time to return to London and my business that Mandy continued to run. I had not made decisions for myself for so long, that the thought of doing so brought me out in a cold sweat. The world seemed a different place to the one I had left all those years ago.

I arrived at the bed and breakfast at almost 5.00 pm and introduced myself to the landlady, Mrs. Roberts. She looked me over, slightly puzzled. She was accustomed to accommodating ex-cons over the years but not one that was dressed so impeccably. Clearly, I was not what she was expecting. I caught sight of my reflection in a large mirror adjacent to the reception desk. I did not look like a convicted murderer just released from a 12-year sentence, but then, what do convicted murderers look like? She was extremely polite and eager to make me feel welcome, and for that I was extremely grateful.

I was shown to my room. It was larger than I thought it would be. Bright green floral curtains matched the general décor. It had an immaculately made double bed with crisp linen sheets and an over-blanket. Other than the bed, the room comprised two bedside tables with a bible placed neatly on one of them. There was a small table and matching green chair and lampshade, and a large wardrobe that dominated the room. I smiled as I thought of Mike's wardrobe all those years ago, full of the finest clothes. This wardrobe would house just one fine suit, a shirt and tie, and a pair of brogues, none of which really belonged to me. There was a door that led to a bathroom. I smiled again. I had my own bath, sink, and toilet and I could use them as often as I liked without seeking permission!

After my induction, which included a list of rules and regulations, Mrs. Roberts told me about the dining arrangements, wished me well, and left. I lay back on the bed, looking forward to supper at 6.30 pm. I stared at the curtains, counting the number of petals on the flowers and promptly fell into a deep sleep.

It was just after 4.00 am when I woke with a start. I was hungry and had missed supper. I had been dreaming about Eleanor's kitchen on the morning I found her dead. Barney was barking in the background. It was a dream I had relived so many times over the years that I had often wondered if I would ever be free of the memory. The house was silent. Breakfast was at 6.30 am so I had over two hours to wait. I knew trying to go back to sleep was pointless, so I got up quietly so as not to disturb the other guests in adjacent rooms. I had bought a newspaper the previous day and set about reading it from cover to cover.

When 6.30 am finally arrived, I tip toed down the stairs to the dining room. I was dressed in the only clothes I had and felt mildly embarrassed that Mrs. Roberts would notice. She greeted me like a long-lost friend. It was such a comforting feeling. The smell of bacon cooking made my mouth water. I sat at my allocated table and pretended to read the same newspaper I had already read several times. It was a while before the other guests appeared. They all acknowledged me with a smile. It all seemed so friendly and vastly different from what I had become accustomed to.

Breakfast over, I carried my empty plate and mug toward the kitchen, a well-rehearsed practice over the years in prison. Mrs. Roberts seemed genuinely touched by my thoughtfulness and commented on it quite loudly. Immediately, another guest who was about to leave collected up his dirty crockery and made his way to the kitchen. She winked at me and whispered, "You've started a trend here, who knows where it will end?"

It is hard to express how much this brief, positive human encounter meant to me. It may seem trivial, but after years of brutal, harsh relationships where I had to be on my guard twenty-four hours a day, where gain and exploitation were the norm, and where there was the constant fear that a word or glance would send out the wrong signals, this seemed so unreal, so perfect.

I returned to my room and set myself some tasks. I was determined to have a list of things to achieve each day. I knew that adjusting to the outside world would take time. The pace of life was hugely different. I had to acquaint myself with everything that was new, just as a child does when first attending school. Liberty is everything, but liberty without structure and objectives to aim for meant nothing. I had heard so many stories in which ex-cons had been released into society without adequate preparation, soon to re-offend or drift into a life of drugs and alcohol abuse, or worse still, commit suicide. I was determined this would not be my fate, but I needed to be vigilant. It was important that I maintained a positive outlook. I was also conscious that over time I would need to surround myself with like-minded people and rediscover my family if I were to have any chance of living a normal life in mainstream society. First, though, there was a big question I needed to address in my quest for normality. Should I be completely honest about my past life with those I met? Despite my instinct telling me to take the honesty route, I knew that announcing I had just served 12 years for murder - a murder I did not commit - would not exactly charm people. At best, it would provide gossip for those seeking attention, while at worst, it would seriously inhibit my ability to integrate. I decided I would need to be circumspect with the truth except with those that had to know.

I started at the bakery. Other than the owner, no one else knew that I had been released from prison. It was good being around people who were working for a living to put food on the table for their families and pay their way in life. My colleagues were not particularly inquisitive about my past, which suited me well. The days drifted into weeks and the weeks into months, and life became as close to a new normal as possible. I had meticulously met all the conditions of my release and integrated into society as best I could. It was challenging and inhibiting but a price worth paying compared to a life behind bars.

I had enjoyed my time in Guildford, but I longed to be back in Winchester. I had changed my name and was now known as *Christopher Jason*. The process of making a name change had not been straightforward, especially as I was now keen to reclaim my assets of the past. Unfortunately, the home I owned in Knightsbridge was not to be a part of those assets. To my dismay, I discovered that an abandoned property is an asset that is turned over to the state after several years of inactivity. Of course, when I failed to return home, went on the run with Peter, then served time in prison, the house had remained empty.

A local, who I was not particularly friendly with, had noticed that the house appeared abandoned. He took the opportunity to maintain the property in a state of repair hoping that if it could be proved that I had died without relatives, or disappeared, he could claim ownership. The law decides when an asset is legally considered abandoned, usually after a period exceeding 2 years. As such, this particular asset – my home - qualified.

Claiming unregistered property or land is not a simple process, nor should it be. A person must first have taken possession of the land, which of course he had. The person must also be able to prove that they have been in *adverse possession* for the required amount of time. Only then are they able to register the asset with the Land Registry. This is exactly what he did.

So, my property was no longer mine and despite my being alive and kicking, I had no recourse to overturn the judgement. I had to let it go. I was not prepared to be subjected to the stress of a long legal fight that I had no chance of winning, nor did I want to attract unwanted attention that would affect my future. The irony was not lost on me. I had been jailed and served a long prison sentence for a crime I did not commit. I had also lost a key asset, my home, for what appeared to be an archaic legal instrument that assumed I was dead. Neither were true. My assets, minus the house that would have been worth more than £2m, amounted to almost £600,000. It was a tidy sum and ignored the value in the business I had. I had forgotten how well off I was.

At the time I met Peter and made the fateful train journey that was to change my life, I was living quite prosperously. I was not a rich man, but neither was I poor. But Winchester drew me in like a magnet, and it was doing so again. I had to return and discover a new life for myself. With a change of name and 12 years of prison etched across my face, it was highly unlikely that I would be noticed as the *Guildford Poisoner,* the name with which the media had branded me, and with which I would have to live for the rest of my life

CHAPTER FIFTEEN - BACK TO

WINCHESTER

It was June 12th, a sunny day with a slight breeze. I packed my meagre possessions and set off for the railway station, destination: *Venta Belgarum*. I sat by the window and watched the countryside unfold before me. It reminded me of Peter and the time we met on the train. Memories flooded back of his life story, the shooting, his escape, and the time we spent avoiding his discovery.

The guard announced that Winchester would be the next stop. I arrived shortly after midday on a crowded train. Now I had some money, I decided to indulge myself for the first month and took a room at The Old Vine under my new name. The OV, as we used to call it, is a public house a stone's throw from the cathedral, with beautifully furnished guest rooms and a fine restaurant. In my past life, I had got to know the owners quite well. They were friends of Andy and Rob at the bookshop, but I felt sure the passing of time would not reveal my real identity. As for Andy and Rob, I was confident they would spot me a mile off, despite having grown a beard and developed the need for glasses since I had last seen them.

I was excited to be back in Winchester and wanted the city to be my permanent home. I was apprehensive too, of the possibility of my identity being discovered, and the complications that may lead to.

I checked in at the OV. The business was indeed under new ownership, and the staff that would come and go, mainly students, were clearly unknown to me. I was relieved. I had asked for room 3. I remembered that when the previous owners had refurbished the property, I was given the opportunity to review the rooms before they were promoted to the public. For me, it was room 3 that had the most appeal.

The Old Vine had been a *drinker's pub* and a few decades earlier, sawdust was spread on the floor daily to soak up the spillage. The air was always smoke-filled. It was legal to smoke in pubs in those days. A certain type of hard drinker frequented the establishment, while the rest of the drinking population in Winchester went elsewhere. The refurbishment was a significant project and took well over a year to complete. It had been a gamble for the owners at the time. Not only were they changing the configuration of the space and investing in restaurant facilities they also rebuilt the top floor and created 8 beautiful guest rooms with antique furniture, high-quality carpets, and lavish curtaining. Anyone who knows anything about marketing would have seen that they were investing in the creation of a new brand to target a different demographic. The question was whether their investment would pay off. Fortunately for them, it had, handsomely.

Having unpacked my entire life's possessions, I drew a bath. It was heaven. I lay there, allowing my mind to wander. I thought about good times past, rather than allowing myself to be consumed by the many skeletons rattling in my closet. I had taken the room for a month, which would take me up to mid-July. That was ample time to plan my life for the following few months at least. Where would I live? I had enough cash to buy a modest property in the town if I chose to. Or perhaps I would rent and avoid the responsibilities of property ownership. After all, it would be a tragedy to go on a long holiday and upon returning, find that it had been acquired by a stranger. The absurdity of the thought amused me. This was an improvement; it failed to do so a few months earlier. But I would leave this decision for another day. I dressed and prepared a list of items I needed to shop for. It was mainly clothes. Those I had were from a charity shop in Guildford. I had kept Mike's white shirt, suit, and brogues, but I had little else. When I had first arrived in town by taxi, a gentleman's clothes shop, oddly named *Eclectic Hound,* caught my eye. It was a two-minute walk from the OV. I decided I would visit first thing in the morning.

I went downstairs for supper. The staff were genuinely friendly and made me feel special. I had become hardened to people with motives of gain and exploitation, corruption and violence and I preferred the *genuinely friendly*. The service and food were superb. I ordered a bottle wine rather than a solitary glass, and as I did, I was transported back to the restaurant in Villiers Street next to Charing Cross Station all those years ago. It was there that I had seen *her,* standing motionless in the rain. I remembered her long black coat with fox brown collar, red umbrella, and lipstick to match.

Prison does not, in my view, rehabilitate people. That is not to say that those perpetrating crimes should not be incarcerated, but if you imprison people and take them off the streets to protect the law-abiding public, a regime needs to be in place to educate, coach, provide mental health therapy, and train inmates so they can eventually return to society, reformed and ready to earn a living. Drug rehabilitation is also a pre-requisite. To do any of this requires a communal change of thinking and adequate investment by government, and that has never been forthcoming, irrespective of political persuasion. Were my musings an unattainable utopia?

Perhaps. I finished a whole bottle of wine and felt liberated. Alcohol fuels creativity and affection in some, and aggression and violence in others. Luckily, I felt more comfortable with the former. I chatted with the staff for a while before returning to my room for a good night's sleep.

I woke with a slight hangover but thought it a worthwhile price to pay for a wonderful first night back in Winchester, and the start of a new life. Breakfast was magnificent and the same staff that had served me at supper were on duty again. I made sure that I expressed my appreciation to them directly. I was offered a choice of dining table in the restaurant if I planned to have supper there that evening, but I politely declined. The city was full of interesting and quirky restaurants and I was keen to explore.

It was time to shop. By the end of the day, I had acquired a decent wardrobe of clothes and all the essentials on my list. Returning to my room, I tried them on. Most were from *Eclectic Hound*. My instinct had been right. The shop had catered for my needs and once again, I had experienced impeccable service from James, the owner.

Over the next couple of weeks, I gave serious thought to my new life and what I would do with it. Winchester was heaving with visitors - mainly groups of overseas tourists. Having left my job at the bookshop after the *hole in the wall* adventure, I was desperate to return to see what had changed. Of course, things are never that easy. I observed the path that led to the bookshop on several occasions, but neither Andy nor Rob turned up. There was a new sign that read 'Antiquarian Bookshop and Famous Medieval tunnel'. I pondered what I should do. I was keen to see Andy and Rob again. After all, I had had a good relationship with them both when I worked there, and we had parted on friendly terms. The elephant in the room, of course, was my trial and incarceration, which I am sure they followed closely as everyone reading newspapers or watching

TV did at the time. What had been their reaction to it all, I wondered? Had they been surprised or shocked by the revelations? Had they believed at the time that I was capable of murder? Prior to the trial and sentencing, Peter's existence in Winchester had been revealed and he had been arrested. That, too, must have reached the attention of Andy and Rob. The only way to find out was visiting the bookshop when they were there. I would return the following day.

I failed to get much sleep that night. I feared they would recoil when they saw me. Perhaps they had sold the business? I waited outside the next morning, before opening time, hoping they would turn up.

It was close to 10.00 am when I caught sight of Andy. I plucked up every ounce of courage and walked into the bookshop. "Hello, Andy. How are you"? He looked me squarely in the face and paused. "Bloody hell, what are you doing here? Are you okay?" His reaction was what I had hoped for. There were a few uncomfortable moments as he questioned whether I had been released from prison or not, but nothing more. It amused me. He must have thought there was a chance I had escaped and returned to Winchester to pick up my final pay packet which, incidentally, they still owed me from 13 years before. Andy had aged well - certainly better than I had.

Having made that initial contact and not been rejected, I offered to leave and catch up some other time, but he was adamant that would not be necessary. He had an assistant who could take over and he insisted we go for a coffee. This was an emotional reunion. He wanted to know everything, literally everything that had happened to me since I left for that fateful Christmas with Eleanor. I told him. The truth poured out of me. It was a cathartic moment; he believed my story – I was sure of that. One can spend a life telling the truth and, consequentially, encounter difficulties and challenges while maintaining integrity. Alternatively, one can live a life of deception and lies that undermine that integrity, and risk losing one's soul. I can live with the former, and I instinctively knew Andy believed I was an innocent man.

My time at the OV had been a good choice and I had found a decent sized terraced cottage to buy. It was perfect, built in 1665, and the owner was keen for a quick sale. I moved in 6 weeks later. Situated on St. Thomas Street, it comprised two delightful oak beamed bedrooms, a study, a small but well-planned bathroom, a good-sized kitchen, sitting room, utility room, small cloakroom, and a tiny but delightful cottage garden. The position was ideal. It was a three-minute walk to the cathedral, the high street and bookshop.

In prison, I had kept in touch as best I could with the outside world and was fascinated by the explosion of online shopping. In fact, online everything. In addition to my love of antiquarian books, I had a passion for antiques, art, and vintage items, on which I had built a business in the past. Once a computer and broadband had been installed in the cottage, I set about selling antiques and art online. At first, it was a challenge without transport. I had not wanted to buy a car as parking was restricted in the area. I agreed with a local van hire firm for them to collect, deliver, and store items for me for a very reasonable price. I went to local auctions and I bought items online. The business quickly took off. It was surprisingly successful. I decided I would not buy and sell old books. That was Andy and Rob's domain, and I would not undermine what they were doing.

In addition to the online success, I secured a part-time job back at the bookshop. Andy's assistant was leaving, and I, Christopher Jason, was offered the job. Like Andy, Rob was supportive and accepted my explanation of the past without hesitation. We were a team again.

The shop layout had changed to accommodate a flow of tourists eager to see the *Monks Tunnel.* Of course, whilst there, they were tempted to buy books. Andy and Rob were now earning a good living working full time and my salary, inflation adjusted, had increased. I was never paid what they owed me from my first stint, but it was of no consequence. What troubled me, however, was the one big lie or deception I had not told them about - my antics in the cellar that had led to the hole in the wall and the revelation of the tunnel. I thought that telling the truth would certainly put my mind at ease but doing so would also undermine the integrity of their business, which had prospered in recent years due to the story of *ghosts of medieval monks* and *the tunnel.*

I had never deliberately lied to them, but I had also not told them the truth, especially about the day that Peter nearly lost his life in the tunnel. I believe there is a distinction between the two, but I would be the first to admit there was a fine line between them.

Summer came and went. Winchester, like London, can be depressing in the winter if you are on your own. By nature, I was a *people watcher.* When I chose not to work, I divided my time between the bookshop and downloading and executing online orders from a bench in the town square, watching the world and his designer dog go by. Frank was a somewhat unique dog, a cockapoo, almost human. He had a knowing look about him and was loved by everyone. I got to know Howard, his owner, well. We enjoyed a regular coffee together. Life was good again.

Apart from Andy and Rob, I fabricated the truth with people all the time. I really had no choice. I felt a sense of loathing when I did stray from the truth, but I knew I had to if I were to protect my future life in Winchester and avoid a painful past that could turn my life upside down. Andy and Rob agreed that I had to invent a past if I were to avoid unnecessary attention. I openly discussed my dilemma and the advice they gave me, which I thought wise, was to fabricate a story and not to deviate from it. It made sense.

I was in good physical health. I took regular exercise whenever I could. The business was doing well, and I could afford the luxury of a gym and tennis club membership, which gave me great pleasure. Tennis had been a passion of mine and the passing of the years had not diminished my competitive spirit. I played in men's doubles matches and joined the singles Box League. I did quite well.

In addition to the gym and tennis, I spent time walking and cycling around the villages that surrounded the city. I knew I had a perfect life under the circumstances, but something was missing: the true intimacy of friendships. There was also *unfinished* business. I had to find out Peter's circumstances. I often wondered if he thought I had forgotten him, and given up his whereabouts to the police? I knew that he had been tried and imprisoned for murdering Mary's husband, but was he still in prison or had he been released? I had to find out and set the record straight.

My research discovered that he was still in prison at HMP Wakefield and was due for parole. I made a visitation request. Four weeks later, I was standing outside the prison gates, looking at the imposing building that housed him. The memories of the day I had left HMP Belmarsh flooded back. I knew what life would be like for inmates behind those gates, especially inmates as sensitive and unworldly as Peter. I dreaded the visit, but it was one I had to make. I needed to clear the air with him. So many emotions, so many questions to ask and answer. I went inside.

As it transpired the visit was a huge relief for me. Peter was delighted I had asked to see him. Other than Mary, who came as often as she could, I was the only other person to do so. I was pleased she had stood by him. I wondered if he would still be alive if she had chosen not to do so. His siblings had chosen to shun him. Peter certainly had the potential to be another suicide statistic.

He put on a brave face for me, but he looked drawn and haggard. He had lost weight he could ill afford to lose. The stresses of everyday life incarcerated in such an environment had quickly taken a toll. There was fear and resignation carved into his face. It creeps into the eyes of inmates, and you can quickly tell whether a man is *the aggressed* or *the aggressor*. The former spent their waking hours in constant fear of what may or may not happen to them. They get used to the humiliating taunts and violent threats that come their way; learning to assimilate rather than react. Violence, when it comes, is swift, often random, and without cause. To retaliate is futile unless you have a death wish, and one tends to have a fair amount of those. You learn to take the beatings and worse. You avoid eye contact and idle conversation, even with people you think you can trust. You learn that trust itself, as well as friendship, are transient commodities that are predicated on a trade. If you have something people want or the power to demand what others have, you gain respect. If, like most inmates, you want to avoid confrontation, serve your term, and return to family and society a reformed character, God help you. It is no mean feat.

My instincts had been right. Peter never knew why I failed to return after Christmas. I was light on detail when I told him I would be away, and he assumed I had abandoned him because of his mental state and gone back to my old life. He had been idly watching TV when he saw a news item about the *Guildford Poisoner* trial and saw a photo of me. He was dumfounded. When the police arrived, he panicked. They searched the apartment and after a short interrogation, he was compelled to confess his identity. The rest was history. I went to great lengths to reassure him that I had not told the police about him, and I was confident he believed me. I explained about Eleanor, the party, and the circumstances following her death. For my own mental health, I needed to know that Peter knew I had not deliberately exposed him, nor did I want him to believe that I was a murderer. On both counts, I was relieved. What remained, as he was reluctant to talk about his time in prison, was his life post incarceration. He was unswervingly committed to Mary and they planned to marry upon his release. Peter spoke of nothing but her and their plans for a life together. Her child was grown up and over the years she had been able to convince him that Peter was a good man. In fact, he had even accompanied her on a few occasions when she visited. On the surface, it seemed that Peter had kept his head above water knowing that Mary was there for him. I knew how difficult it was to adapt to life back in society and the challenges it could present, but this was not the time to talk about the subject. He needed to sustain that feeling of belonging to someone. The future, and whatever it may hold, could wait.

After we had said our goodbyes, I left the prison gates, turning once more to face the huge architectural monstrosity of a building, before heading back to the railway station. Prison buildings are primarily designed to keep people in, but they also convey enough power, authority and fear for most people to want to stay on the outside.

On the train back, I reflected on my visit. At first, when I had sat opposite Peter, conversation was stilted. I talked openly and honestly about the circumstances of the events leading up to and following my time in prison, and he had begun to relax. That state of relaxation soon turned to excitement, leading me to worry about how stable he was, mentally. Prison life affects people in different ways. For hardened criminals, it is an opportunity to assert their power and influence almost at any cost. For others, the stresses and strains of life inside can break them. Despite Mary being there for him when he came out, I feared for his future. I was determined I would not abandon him. It was a pledge I had made years earlier but had failed to keep.

101

CHAPTER SIXTEEN - NOT

FORGETTING PETER

My circle of acquaintances grew in Winchester. Deliberately avoiding the bond of friendship that often came with those encounters was hard. Getting close to people had always come naturally to me. I had never felt alone, truly alone, until prison changed my life forever. A trained psychologist or even a casual observer could see that my thoughts and actions were dominated by past events. Everything I did or said was carefully scripted. I judiciously avoided eggshells placed in my path. I could not relax or be myself.

My time with Peter at HMP Wakefield, and the conversation we had had, kept returning to my mind. I waited to hear from him about his release date, but nothing came. I had offered to be there with Mary when he got out. I knew from my own experience how important it was to have people who genuinely cared about you, offering support at that crucial time. Mrs. Roberts, my landlady in Guildford, had been there for me and I knew I would be eternally grateful. I did not have Mary's contact details to make enquiries, so I called the prison office for an update. Of course, I knew that only registered family members or legal representatives were able to be informed about a prisoner's status but thought it worth a try. I applied for another visitation order, but it was declined for no apparent reason. It was extremely difficult getting any sense out of the authorities.

I wrote to Peter, and three weeks later, I heard back from him. The handwriting on the envelope told its own story. It was an unsteady hand that had painstakingly formed the shape of every character of every word. People rarely used pens anymore, especially fountain pens to write letters. Everything is typed and computer generated, pushing handwritten letters into obscurity. People who chose to write letters nowadays were either adept at the skill, often shunning the computer altogether, or inexperienced in the art but lacking any alternative. In Peter's case, it was the latter. Having opened the envelope and carefully placed it to one side, I straightened the uneven creases on the page and started to read. His handwriting was uncontrolled. It slanted to the right and he mixed upper and lower-case letters in many words. Punctuation was missing and the grammar was poor, but none of that mattered. I had kept few handwritten letters in my life. Those that I had kept have special significance and meaning, becoming treasures I would never part with whilst I was alive. Peter's letter would join them. For reasons he failed to make clear, Mary had stopped visiting. She had not responded to his letters or 'phone calls. Without Mary as his rock, he now had nothing: nothing to look forward to, nothing to live for. He had a daily routine to keep safe. He had avoided any form of disagreement or confrontation and always did what was asked of him by the prison guards. The only indulgence he had was thinking about Mary, her next visit, and the life they had planned together after his release.

Life in prison, especially long-term sentences, can destroy a person's will to live, unless they have strategies to combat the negative mental strain, as well as future goals and ambitions to aim for. In Peter's case, he was consumed by Mary and everything was tied up in their future happiness. Without her, a spiral of melancholy awaited him, or worse.

His account of himself, his thoughts, and his feelings of loss for Mary had led to an attempted suicide. It had failed, but only when a guard had found him on his cell floor having cut his wrists. He was bleeding to death and was admitted to the infirmary for treatment and mental rehabilitation. Weeks later, he was re-introduced to his cell and depression had set in. It did not go unnoticed. He was taunted by other inmates, eager to exploit his vulnerability. Uncharacteristically, having entered the dining room for breakfast one morning, he attacked one of the bullies with a penknife he had found in his cell a few weeks before. His frenzied attack badly cut the persons face and hands and during his restraint, he wounded a prison guard. His uncontrolled actions placed him in solitary confinement before being moved to another wing of the prison, where the toughest inmates resided. He was not returned to a psychiatric ward as he should have been. Instead, he was left to wait for the hearing that would determine his suitability for parole. He knew it would be out of the question and an extension of his prison term was inevitable.

I cannot put into words the emotion he was clearly suffering, or the hopelessness of his dilemma after being jilted by Mary. He was not the most articulate of people, but every word conveyed in his letter was carefully and deliberately chosen. It provided a powerful account of his mental state at the very moment he wielded the knife. His actions were premeditated in that he chose to carry it to the dining hall and, when given the opportunity, had harmed one of his aggressors, but I would argue that he should have been receiving psychiatric treatment in his mental state. He should never have been returned to his cell.

Actions of this kind, attacking another prisoner, were totally out of character for the Peter I knew, but what the incident did demonstrate was that his instinct was to lose total control in the face of extreme anger, frustration, and fear. That much had been true when he shot Mary's husband. Most people have the capacity to draw a line, to quantify how far they would go to seek revenge, but not people wired like Peter. The distinction between a psychopath and someone like Peter, is that the former has no remorse for their actions. Peter's remorse would haunt him for the rest of his life. He had become blinded by a light triggered in his head: the *fight or flight* instinct, over which he had no influence.

I knew that when he was eventually released from prison, assuming he resisted harming himself or indeed harming others, he would be a damaged human being. As much as I wanted to see him adapt to a normal life on the outside, I feared he would be unable to adjust. His prospects for the future looked bleak.

I vowed I would maintain contact and was prepared to modify my own life to help Peter when he was released.

CHAPTER SEVENTEEN - A

KNOCK ON THE DOOR

There was a persistent knock at the door. I had planned to fix the doorbell ever since I moved into the cottage, but like so many other practical jobs around the house, it was destined to wait. I never had visitors, so I was intrigued. I assumed it was someone trying to sell me something. I opened the door and for a split second, I thought I saw Eleanor standing before me. I was unable to speak. It was not Eleanor. It was her twin sister, Caroline. I was shocked to see her, especially after the hostility she had shown toward me all those years ago. Why was she here? How did she get my address? I invited her in.

When I knew I was due to be released from prison, I decided to write a letter to one of Eleanor's cousins, Grace. I had a good relationship with her, as the only person who believed at the time that I was innocent of Eleanor's murder. I told her confidentially of my plan to return to Winchester and suggested, at some point, we should meet up. Apparently, that letter had been shared with Caroline who, having visited friends in the area, thought she would look me up.

It was an uncomfortable first few minutes as we exchanged pleasantries. There was no mention of Eleanor, our soured relationship, or my imprisonment. It seemed obvious to me that she was unsettled or worried about something and I encouraged her to tell me what it was.

She lived in South Africa and had spent limited time in England in recent years. Her married name was Caroline De Jong. She had been married to a corrupt South African politician, who she had recently divorced. For some days, she had been followed by people she knew had the intention of harming her. I persuaded her that she was safe and suggested that she slept in the spare room until morning. I was curious and wanted to know more, but I would wait. I knew her, but at the same time, I knew nothing of her.

It was almost 2.00 pm the following day before she woke and crept into my study. I was completely unaware of her presence until I turned my chair to reach for a book and she was there, watching me. I was shocked to see her. It seemed strange because I had thought of nothing else since her dramatic entrance the previous evening. She looked serene. The pained expression on her face from yesterday had gone. She smiled but said nothing. I rose from my chair and offered a short embrace. She accepted. I was keen to find out why she was in trouble, and with whom. I did not have to wait long to find out.

I learned that she had been followed for days by men who knew she had in her possession diamonds she had smuggled into the UK from Zimbabwe. Her grandparents had owned a large farm in Bulawayo, in the north-east of the country, but they had then been killed by a gang of farm workers, egged on by the military. According to other local white farmers and friends who had witnessed the tragedy, some of those responsible had worked on the farm for generations and had been treated like family. All the same, they had shown no compunction in setting the house and outbuildings alight.

Caroline's mother and father had also perished in the fire; they were visiting at the time. Apparently, she had always been closer to her grandparents than her parents although I failed to ask why. She was in Cape Town lecturing at the University when she took a call from a friend and received the news. She returned to what was left of her grandparent's farmhouse to find everything had perished or been looted.

A week or so after the funeral of her family, she went back to the house one last time, and discovered a smoke-charred safe that had been partly buried in the rubble. It had originally been concealed in a wall, so nobody outside the family would know of its whereabouts. She was close to her grandfather and he had told her the safe's code in case of an emergency. With that knowledge, she opened it to find personal items, a little money, and a large bag of uncut diamonds, crudely tied up with string. She knew her grandfather had invested money in diamonds over the years as an insurance policy, just in case the economy declined, or worse still, the political situation became unstable and the currency became worthless. How wise he had been.

Later, surprised to discover the diamonds in the bag were of the finest quality and not knowing what to do with them, she decided to conceal them in her suitcase and travel to London to visit an acquaintance she hardly knew, just to escape and give her time to think.

Months passed, and with no real home to return to in Africa, she decided to remain in London and rent an apartment. She communicated on a regular basis with close friends in Harare and when she received an invitation to their wedding, she returned, leaving the diamonds hidden in her flat. Her intention was to sell them in the UK, but she was unsure how to go about doing it.

It was at that wedding she met Richard, the brother of Abigail, a girlfriend she had known for some time. He was much older than Abigail, and despite Caroline visiting their farm on a regular basis, she had never met him. He was immediately flirtatious with her and questioned her about her family. She later discovered that he had moved to South Africa and started an export business. He claimed he knew her grandfather through his business connections, which seemed odd to her; after all, what would her grandfather have to do with an export company when he sold everything the farm produced to local markets? That said, she was flattered by his attention and, feeling quite low after the death of her family, she needed little persuasion to engage in a close and passionate encounter.

Having pre-booked a non-refundable flight to London three days later, she had the dilemma of returning on that flight or choosing to stay with him in his Harare apartment. She chose the latter.

A few extra days turned into three weeks. They enjoyed every minute together and spent little if any time apart. It was early on a Thursday morning that Richard took a 'phone call that changed everything. Up until that point he had been jovial and flirtatious, but his mood changed after the call. Something had panicked him, and Caroline knew it. Without much explanation, he said he needed to go to Cape Town and would return two days later. She asked if she could accompany him, but he dismissed her offer. Hurriedly, he packed a bag and left. She spent the rest of the day confused, trying to work out why he had appeared so worried.

Despite enjoying her time with him, she thought she should go back to London. She was concerned he was making assumptions about their relationship and planning a future together, which made her feel uncomfortable. She was not ready to commit herself to a long-term relationship after a messy divorce.

The following morning, she 'phoned the airline to book her flight to London for the Sunday evening. She wanted to leave on an early flight but felt she had to stay until Richard returned to say goodbye. The whole of Friday was spent shopping and making 'phone calls to friends across Africa before her departure. At about 6.15 pm, the 'phone rang. Expecting it to be him, she lifted the receiver, but the line went quiet. The caller hung up. Again, the 'phone rang, and again she answered, but the same thing happened. Several hours later, it rang again. This time, she left it ringing, knowing that any message would be recorded on the voicemail. The caller was brief, and to the point.

"This is your final warning, Richard. Your last chance. You have until midnight on Sunday to sort things out. If you let me down, you know the consequences." This was no idle threat. Something was terribly wrong.

Her original plan after the family funeral, when she had first met Richard, was to discover what he knew about her grandfather. That plan had evaporated after their first night together. Without knowing when he would return, and without a mobile number or address at which to contact him, she was incapable of passing this message on. For several hours, she tried to get in touch with Abigail to see if she had a contact number for him, but her 'phone rang continuously. Eventually, she went to bed, fully expecting a call from Richard to wake her. It never came.

It was late Saturday morning when she woke. She felt tired after a disturbed night's sleep worrying about the message. Over and over, she played it in her head, until she had invented a hundred interpretations of its meaning. Richard was in trouble - of that there was little doubt. In getting out of bed, she knocked over a glass of wine on the dressing table and its contents ran into the top drawer. She rushed into the bathroom for tissues to mop it up. When she opened the drawer, she saw the corner of a bag identical to the one she had recovered from her grandfather's safe, it was partly concealed and tied at the neck with string. She quickly closed the drawer and sat back on the bed. A moment passed before her curiosity invited her to take another look. She reopened the drawer and carefully removed the bag. Slowly, she untied the string and poured the contents onto the bed. The bag contained dozens of diamonds of a similar size and quantity to those she had recovered from her grandfather's. Confused, she tried to make a connection between Richard, her grandfather, the diamonds, and the message on the voicemail. Was there even one? Was her grandfather buying diamonds from Richard? Had her grandfather paid for the diamonds she had found? Perhaps not, and the original supplier wanted the money or the diamonds back, but Richard was unable to provide them? Her thoughts then turned to her first encounter with him, when he had swept her off her feet. Richard knew her grandfather had been murdered and he also knew she had recovered the diamonds and he was incredibly inquisitive.

What was he planning? Was his affection just a part of a wider plot to recover them? She felt panicked.

Again, she tried to recall everything Richard had said to her during their time together. She decided he had manipulated her from the start and his motive all along had been to steal or somehow acquire the diamonds she possessed. The implicit threat in the voicemail message would certainly have worried him. For all his charm and apparent confidence, there lurked inside a vulnerable man, unprepared for threats of this nature - or so she believed. There was only one thing for her to do. She had to pack a few essentials and leave the apartment as quickly as possible. Nervously, she started to gather her things when the 'phone rang. Rooted to the spot, she waited for the voicemail to click in after a few rings. "Caroline. Are you there?" It was Richard. His voice was strained and tense. It was obvious something was wrong. "Look I'll be back within the hour. It's 10.23 am, if you pick up this message before I get back, wait for me in the apartment…its important." Determined to leave before he returned, she rushed to finish packing, then checked over the apartment once more before opening the door. For a split second, she stopped dead in her tracks. Should she take the bag of diamonds with her? Something in her mind told her to do so. She turned, rushed back to the bedroom, and removed the bag from the drawer, placing it in her coat pocket. On her way out, she spotted Richard's car keys and pocketed them, too. Panic and guilt simultaneously overwhelmed her. She struggled to comprehend what was happening.

Once outside the apartment, she quickly looked across the corridor and down the stairs to see if her exit was clear. She had chosen not to use the elevator, thus avoiding the possibility that Richard would return early and intercept her. She could not risk it. Suitcase in hand, she made straight for the stairs. A man was walking down the corridor toward her. She knew he was a resident. There were three flights of stairs to negotiate. The suitcase was relatively light. She had only packed a few basic items knowing she would never see the rest of her belongings again. At every level, she stopped to see her exit was clear. The journey to the car park, which ordinarily took but a few minutes, seemed like hours. By now, she was shaking with trepidation. She loaded the suitcase onto the back seat of Richard's car and threw her jacket on top of it, double-checking to see that the bag containing the diamonds was still in her pocket. She got into the driver's seat and closed the door. The silence was deafening. She stared through the windscreen. *What now?* she thought. Sensibly, she decided to move the car out of the car park to a point opposite the apartment block, so she could watch for Richard to return. A side street with full view of its entrance was an ideal observation post where she would not be seen. Richard had taken a taxi when he left. An hour and a half passed, and he had not arrived. By now, she had calmed down. It was nearly twenty minutes to one when a cab drew up outside the apartment block opposite, and Richard got out. He paid the driver and hurried into the building. Now she knew where he was, she needed to decide her next move.

The bedroom of the apartment faced onto the street and within moments of him entering the building, she saw him walk past the bedroom window. He must have sprinted to the apartment, assuming she would be in there. As her gaze remained on the window, she was startled by the ringtone on her mobile phone. She reached into her pocket to retrieve it. As she was about to press the call receive button, she hesitated, believing it to be Richard. She switched it off.

How had he got her mobile number? She had no recollection of giving it to him. Minutes later, she changed her mind and switched the phone on. Immediately, she received a message. "Caroline, where are you? I asked you to wait for me at the apartment. Call me back on my mobile when you receive this message". His tone was assertive.

No sooner had she listened to the voicemail than the 'phone rang again. She took the call this time. "Caroline, is that you?" "Yes." "Where are you? I thought I asked you to wait in the apartment for me?" "David, what's going on?" There was a brief pause before he answered. "Going on...what do you mean? Caroline, can you please tell me where you are?" By now, her patience was wearing thin. Despite her attempts to end the call, Richard insisted on interrogating her. Her mind raced with confusion. "I'm at the airport about to board a flight". He was shocked to hear she was heading for London and was intending to get on the next flight. He begged her to wait until he got to the airport to discuss the diamonds she had taken from his chest of drawers. Had she been too quick to draw conclusions about him and the diamonds? Was he telling the truth and she had foolishly taken his property? She could not take the risk of finding out and was not prepared to wait for him.

"What flight did you say you were on?" The slow and deliberate tone of his voice made her raise her eyes in the direction of the bedroom window. There, she saw him staring directly at her. "Why are you sitting in my car, Caroline?" The 'phone line suddenly went dead, and he disappeared from the window. She knew he was on his way down to her. She fumbled with the keys to make a getaway. Wracked with anxiety, she turned the key, but the engine failed to start. She pumped the accelerator with all her might and the engine turned once more. Again, it failed to respond. By now, Richard was running at full speed from the apartment block toward the car. On the third attempt, the engine started. Adrenalin pumping, she rammed the car in first gear and with squealing tires, she pulled out into the road, narrowly missing his arm as he stretched out to stop her. Looking in the rear-view mirror, she saw him standing stationary in the middle of the road, his arms held high.

His outline shrank into the distance as she continued to drive. A few minutes later, she stopped, reached across to the passenger seat, and turned her 'phone off. It was several minutes before she was able to regain her composure. Convinced he would have prevented her from leaving and that her safety was in jeopardy, she decided to head for Harare airport. She would wait there until she could get a flight to London.

CHAPTER EIGHTEEN –

CAROLINE'S ESCAPE TO

LONDON

The road signs to the airport indicated seven miles to go. As her mind played out the events of the past twenty-four hours, she grew surer that she had made the right decision to escape Richard and began to relax. She parked his car in the short-term car park, a short walk from the terminal. He had no chance of finding it. If things went wrong inside, at least she would only have a short distance to go to retrieve it.

The airport was busy. The departures board indicated that a direct flight to London via British Airways was due to leave in just over three hours. There was a long queue at the BA service desk and for a while, she feared she would not get a ticket. She lined up behind a family with several huge suitcases. The mother and father looked pensive as if they too were being pressured to seek a new life elsewhere. Political turmoil in the country was worsening by the day, and those that had the opportunity to leave the country were doing so. Their three young children bounded with excitement at the thought of the journey ahead. Her mind wandered back to her childhood on the farm and thoughts of her parents. They were carefree days, long gone.

The queue slowly shortened. Reaching into her pocket, she took out her mobile phone, switched it on, and received a voicemail. It was Richard.

"Caroline, I know what you've done. You have stolen the diamonds from my drawer. Why did you do it? I must have them back. I beg you not to do anything stupid. Please call me when you receive this message. You must call me, Caroline, you must call me!"

In her desperation to escape, she had completely forgotten the diamonds in her pocket. She knew there was a huge risk in boarding a plane with contraband as she had done on her flight to London. She had been lucky on that occasion not to be stopped and searched, but could she take a risk a second time? The futility of her wait in the queue became apparent. She just could not risk it. She needed time to collect her thoughts and stepped away from the queue.

It was obvious after their earlier conversation on the phone that Richard knew she was heading for the airport. The unanswered question was how long would it take for him to get there? It was crucial that she boarded the London bound flight; after all, where else could she go? The big question was deciding what to do with the diamonds. She had totally discounted the idea of trying to smuggle them aboard. Detection systems were highly sophisticated, and security was on high alert after recent terrorist attacks at major airports. Even if she were successful in getting them to London, there was always the risk that customs would search her, and the penalty for diamond smuggling was severe.

She knew she could not carry off the deception a second time. The guilt would be writ large on her face from the moment she checked in. There had to be another way. Walking aimlessly around the concourse, it came to her. The only way she could board the plane was to put them in a safety deposit box. She recalled seeing a sign earlier for long-term storage and headed in that direction. Having deposited them in one of the boxes and put the key in her pocket, she hurried back to the check-in desk. The queue was longer than before, and the chance of obtaining a ticket even more unlikely.

Richard knew she planned to board a plane for London, so it was inevitable he would head for the check-in desk at precisely the point where she was standing. The crassness of the situation was not lost on her.

As she finally reached the front of the queue, the moment of truth arrived. The flight was full. Her desperate plea to buy a ticket failed. The next flight would leave at 6.00 am the following morning. She had no choice. She bought a ticket and decided to wait it out.

With the diamonds safely deposited, her priority was now to disappear until the morning. When Richard arrived at the airport, he would try to establish if she had already boarded a plane or checked in for another flight, but she knew the airlines were not at liberty to disclose personal information.

She felt a sense of relief, but the same challenge remained. Could she avoid him seeing her before she could board the plane in the morning knowing he might remain at the airport? After the drama of the past twenty-four hours, she was exhausted. Her emotions had been dragged in all directions and sleep deprivation was catching up on her. Purposefully, she made her way to the exit and the taxi rank. It was too dangerous to stay at the airport. The thought of sleeping on a chair in some discrete corner and being suddenly woken by Richard had no appeal. Within the hour, she had checked into an airport hotel, showered, and was in bed on the outer edges of a deep sleep. The phone rang. In an instant, she lifted the receiver to be told it was 4.30 am. It felt as though she had only just closed her eyes. She had half an hour to shower, dress, and make her way back to the airport. Her main concern, though, was not being seen during any part of the short journey. If she could make it to the security check-in area, she would be safe. The taxi stopped at the edge of the drop off area and she paid the fare and hurried through the revolving door. She had to remain vigilant.

There was little doubt in her mind that Richard would already have been to the airport in search of her. The question was whether he had given up and returned to the apartment, or if he had remained at the airport, knowing the first flight out was 6.00 am believing she might be on it. She feared the latter was more than a possibility. After all, she had the diamonds, and he was not about to give them up.

With ticket clutched in hand, she moved slowly but deliberately toward the international departures gate, keeping a watchful eye on those around her. The airport was less busy today, which made her more conspicuous. She knew her fate would be determined in the minutes ahead.

The journey was a short and tense one, with every step feeling as though she were walking a tightrope without a security net. She reached the security desk and ran her fingers nervously through her hair. She was desperate to glance around to see if the coast was clear, but too fearful in case Richard was there, staring straight at her. She fumbled nervously as she presented her boarding pass to the security officer. Where was her passport? It was gone. She looked to the floor and searched her pockets several times as people lined up behind her. From a distance, an elderly man could be heard calling her name. As he approached the security desk, his voice became louder. The passport was held high above his head, his hand waving to attract attention. It was precisely the kind of attention she was keen to avoid.

Her emotions swung from elation, having discovered that the passport had been found, to absolute horror at her name being broadcast for everyone to hear. People turned around to see what the fuss was all about.

If she were to be discovered by Richard, it would be now. Thrilled the old man had been of service, he then proceeded to explain to Caroline in minute detail that he had seen her drop the passport and had retrieved it. The line of people behind her became agitated as the security officer waited patiently for him to hand it over. Turning to face the old man, she smiled and prayed for the handover to be complete. Eventually, he thrust the passport into her hand. At that precise moment, she heard her name broadcast aloud once more. This time, the voice was Richard's.

Before she could rush through security, he grabbed her by the arm. People in the queue retreated immediately, anticipating trouble. She screamed, but the louder she did, the more forceful Richard became. As he attempted to drag her away from the line, several airport staff came to her aid and wrestled him away from her. Confusion ensued as he proclaimed loudly that she had stolen something from him. She remained silent, looking for an opportunity to escape. Security guards and police swiftly arrived, subduing Richard. Then, at just the right moment, when everyone's attention was focused on him, she slipped through a gap in the crowd and made her way to the nearest exit. She glanced back, but eyes were not on her.

Outside the airport building, she dashed to a taxi stand and within seconds, she was being driven away from the scene and back to the hotel where she had slept the previous night. Fortunately, she had retrieved her passport from the clutches of airport security before the incident and placed it in her pocket next to the safety deposit box key. The drama of the past couple of days caught up with her. She arrived back at the hotel lobby extremely tired, as though she had been up all night. What next? She felt alone and isolated. Like it or not, she had to return to the airport to recover the diamonds and she still desperately needed to leave the country. Not knowing what happened to Richard after she escaped put her at a disadvantage. Were the police looking for her? She still had her passport, but would she be able to exercise her right to leave the country without being stopped? She was trapped and had to find a way to return to London. The best chance of avoiding detection, she thought, would be to board a plane at a different international airport.

Having showered and eaten a meal in the room, she dressed and went down to the lobby. Carrying the small bag of belongings that she had hurriedly packed in Richard's apartment she approached the checkout desk to settle her bill.

Within the hour, she had hired the cheapest car she could find and was heading south toward Bulawayo, where she planned to catch a flight to Johannesburg and then onto London. This was proving to be a costly journey in more ways than one.

It was an extremely hot day and the air conditioning in the car failed to work within minutes of her driving it away from the rental agency. Her grandfather had instilled in her *that the cheapest was not necessarily best value for money* and had always encouraged her to be objective when buying anything. Of course, he was right. She recalled the last time she had seen her parents and grandparents and spent quality time with them. Tears welled up in her eyes. She was sitting on the verandah listening to the animals in the bush as the sun began to set. The sunsets there were spectacular. The sun was so huge that it almost consumed the entire sky, and darkness would come quickly. This was the time when the big cats came alive and their predatory skills came to the fore. It was a magical day when everything seemed to be in place. Her grandparents had returned from vacation in Europe and were relaxed and happy together as they had always been. They had shared every moment together since they first met at the age of fifteen. After drinks and watching the sunset, they went in for dinner and were joined by close friends John and Alex, who lived ten kilometers away. They recounted their vacation in such graphic terms. Everyone was astonished at how they remembered the minutest detail of every minute of every day. As the evening wore on and the alcohol took effect, her grandfather announced, somewhat emotionally, that he was planning to retire. With the political situation deteriorating, they felt the time was right to sell up and move to Europe. They had wanted to settle in London, but the weather and exchange rates dictated that Italy would probably be their best bet. She was saddened that the farm would be sold on and it would mark the end of an era, but she was also happy that they would at last be able to step back from all the hard work of running the farm and make the most of their retirement. They had always wanted to travel. John and Alex were not surprised by the news. In fact, they too had considered selling up their wholesale business in town and emigrating, but their business partners would not pay them the true value of their shares, fearful that if they left, the business would decline. So, they had resigned themselves to staying on.

At almost two thirty in the morning, Caroline went to bed and slept until late morning. By the time she rose, her grandfather had been working on the farm for some hours and her grandmother had baked bread and cakes for later in the day. After lunch and a catch-up on local news, they sat outside to enjoy the breeze. It was a vivid memory of happy family life, one that was becoming increasingly rare as the country declined into anarchy.

A bump in the road shook her from her memories. Hours had passed with only the occasional car moving in the opposite direction. Dog tired and too hot to carry on, she stopped at the side of the road. Within an instant, she was asleep.

The wind kicked up dust from the road, which carried through the open window onto her face. Startled, she woke. She had been asleep for over an hour and it took her a few moments to remember where she was. She was hungry and thirsty but decided to press on to Bulawayo without any further stops. Two hours later, she approached the outer perimeter of the town traffic. She felt relieved that she had made the journey without incident, but still felt vulnerable at the thought of boarding the flight to Johannesburg.

It was late afternoon when she dropped the hire car off and made her way into the terminal building. Glancing around, satisfied she was safe, she went directly to the ticket desk. There was a forty-minute wait for the plane and only a further one hour at Johannesburg airport for the onward flight to London. The first flight took one hour twenty minutes and on the longer flight to London, she had an aisle seat next to two elderly sisters, who were returning to the UK for the first time in thirty years. Both were eager to make her acquaintance but having settled, she slept for most of the journey, only waking as the plane began to land.

As they touched down at Heathrow airport, she felt refreshed and relaxed. She had avoided Richard and managed to get to London. Oddly, though, she still felt concerned for him. A great deal of what she knew of the situation was speculation. If her assumptions were true, he could be in serious difficulty. Meanwhile, the diamonds sat in the strong room at Harare airport, under her control but out of her reach.

Safely through immigration, she collected her belongings and made her way to customs. She was nervous. There was just one immediate obstacle to overcome. She faced the double opaque glass doors leading to the Arrivals Hall. She breezed through customs without an officer in sight. The moment had arrived. She walked, head slightly bowed along the roped off concourse, with an audience of people staring at her. The pathway seemed never ending. All she wanted to do was disappear into the crowd.

As she made her way to the exit, she spotted two sinister looking men watching her every move. They followed her. She joined a queue waiting for a taxi. When her turn came, she quickly jumped into a cab and sped away into central London.

CHAPTER NINETEEN -

CONFESSIONS

Her story was believably detailed, and I had no reason to doubt the authenticity of what she had told me. What remained unanswered was why she had decided to contact me of all people. I thought I was the last person she would want to see again. We had so much bad history. According to her, I had deprived her of the close relationship she had craved with her sister when they were growing up, I had had an affair with Eleanor just prior to her marrying Mike, and, I had murdered her twin, her only sister. How could she possibly forgive me?

I had not left the house since she had arrived. I made breakfast and she seemed aloof. The unanswered questions remained. I wanted to know: Why call on me? I had virtually run out of groceries and suggested I should venture out.

Two minutes into the journey and the heavens opened. The supermarket was a ten- minute walk away. Very few people were out and those that were had the sense to dress appropriately. I was beginning to relax into a steady walk when I caught sight of two men on the opposite side of the road, dressed in black raincoats. They looked in my direction and I sensed a problem. My anxiety was short-lived, though, as they soon walked away in the direction of the cottage. Then, it dawned on me. If they were the men Caroline had been talking about, perhaps they followed me for a short distance, only to return to the cottage, knowing Caroline was alone. Was I being paranoid?

If I returned immediately and my theory was wrong, I would seem foolish and cause Caroline to worry. But then, if I continued to the store and returned to find that she had been abducted or, worse still, was lying dead, how would I be able to live with myself? The supermarket was just a few minutes away. I concluded that my imagination had run riot and it would be best if I pressed on with the shopping as quickly as I could. I sped around the aisles, grabbing anything that looked remotely familiar. I felt uneasy. My inclination was to run back as fast as I could, but carrying the shopping made it impossible. As I approached the cottage, I glanced around but there was no sign of anyone. I let myself in. As I dragged the shopping into the kitchen I called out for Caroline and she came down the stairs. I felt foolish and said nothing of my paranoia.

We talked for most of the evening. She told the story of her grandparents, the farm, Richard, the men following her, and the diamonds in such detail that her story simply had to be true. We agreed it made no sense for her to rush back to London the following day.

She had arrived with only a few clothes. We would go into town to do some shopping in the morning. I was due a shift at the bookshop. I called Andy first thing to see if I could be excused, he was fine about it. I took Caroline a cup of tea. I liked the idea of fussing over her. She seemed relaxed. We had breakfast and walked into town. I just loved the cottage being so central. Everything was so close to hand.

I asked if she wanted me to accompany her into the shops, but she wanted to shop alone. I was disappointed but understood. I returned to the cottage and waited for her to return. She bought quite a lot of quality casual wear, which I thought was a good sign. Perhaps she would stay longer than I imagined?

She changed her clothes, choosing a pair of jeans and sweater to wear. She looked terrific and reminded me so much of Eleanor. They looked very much alike, although they were not identical twins and had vastly different personalities. Eleanor was warm, thoughtful, kind, loving, emotional. Caroline was cool, calm, and collected. She was more analytical and controlling.

We returned to town for a coffee. She told me more about her life in Zimbabwe and lecturing in Cape Town. I had visited South Africa on many occasions during my travels. I loved the beauty of the country. I had been to Kruger game reserve on safari and taken the blue train from Johannesburg to Cape Town. From there, I had flown to East London and Port Elizabeth. She, too, had been to Kruger, and of course knew Cape Town well.

In the café, we talked a lot. All was going reasonably well until she wanted to know more about my time with Eleanor that Christmas day, and what had truly happened to her. I suppose it was obvious she would enquire at some point. Truth be told, I was surprised she had waited until now. A sinking feeling descended upon me, although I had learnt how to mask the facial expression that accompanied that feeling.

Pouring out a catalogue of lies, or, as I tried to justify it to myself, the *manufactured truth,* was mentally draining. Over time, though, thinking on my feet had become easier, especially around those with whom I only had a superficial relationship. Of course, it was different with someone like Caroline. What to say, and how to say it? Andy and Rob had given me some sage advice which resonated. *'If you have to fabricate the truth, find a story and stick to it.'* It made sense in theory, but the variables involved in successfully carrying it off made it impossible to execute. Human beings are anything but predictable, at least in their questioning. If I could have given Caroline a list of questions to ask, I would have been able to prepare the answers, as one does for an examination at school, to satisfy her curiosity. Unfortunately, that is not how it works! I had to answer her questions, but I had to avoid saying anything that may lead her to believing I had killed Eleanor.

Was I married? Did I have a partner? The simple and honest answer was *no* to both questions. She knew I had children. She would have followed all the media stories at the time about my alleged guilt, but what did she really think, what did she believe? The fact she was here with me now suggested she was not fearful of me.

It was a difficult conversation. Understandably, she was eager to hear my side of the story. It reminded me of the interrogation Judge Lucy had given me at Jack's Christmas party, when she had shoved me onto the sofa. Of course, the circumstances were different now. There was no frivolity, no fun, just direct questions about that fateful day. Truth be told, I had no idea what she thought of my story relating to the events as I recalled them. I was conscious that my eyes veered away from her too frequently and that was a bad sign, one that could be interpreted as guilt. I knew I had to do better.

I was pleased she had turned up on my doorstep to tell her story. My pleasure did not extend to revealing my memories of that day, though. I had rehearsed it so many times in my head. I wanted to always be able to recount the events in the minutest of detail, so that I could convince even the most cynical listener.

We returned to the cottage without saying a word. I could have asked her if she believed my story, but I thought it wrong to do so. That was a judgement she would have to make for herself. Again, she had come to me, not the other way round. If she thought me capable of murdering her sister, would she not be fearful of her own life? Entering the cottage, I offered to make some tea, but she declined and said she wanted to rest. She went to the spare room and I heard her making 'phone calls but I wasn't about to listen in. It was early evening when she emerged.

She was pleasant enough, but I now sensed she did not believe what I had told her. It was awkward. I had no option but to ask her directly. Her response was unexpected. She failed to understand how a jury had found me guilty. She nor other members of her family attended the trial.

She continued to question me, this time about my life more generally. I told her about the London business that Mandy ran for me. I told her about my part-time work at the bookshop and finding the tunnel. I told her about the online business I had started and how it was flourishing. Now, I had arrived at that defining point, the point of no return, the crossroads where the choice was simple: *lies and deceit,* or the *unadulterated truth?*

In front of me, immersed in my storytelling, was a woman I was growing fond of as I had with her sister, although I knew my feelings were not reciprocated - at least not yet. I felt I wanted her to be a part of my future life. Someone had said to me years earlier that life can be summed up as a *sequence of random events.* At the time, it seemed too simplistic a notion, but the more I thought about it, the more I came to agree. So far, my life reflected the meaning of those five words. Meeting Peter, Eleanor, incarceration, the bookshop, and now Caroline. This was the sequence of random events that made up the very fabric of who I was, the life I had experienced and,

I hoped, the life that lay ahead. I delivered my story as though I were acting out a well-rehearsed script from a stage play. It was word perfect. It was an academy performance. It was a liberating experience. I barely drew breath throughout. Caroline listened, motionless but not spellbound. Apart from Andy and Rob and, more recently, Peter, I did not dare tell a soul about my past. Now, I had added Caroline to my inner circle of confidants. As I did, a huge weight that had burdened my mind for so long was lifted. I had told the truth about my past. The unadulterated truth.

I had experienced so many emotional turning points in recent years, both uplifting and horrific, and had become accustomed to their outcomes. But for me, the importance of honesty with close personal relationships was still something I held most dear. I was so relieved that Caroline had stayed. I wanted to share a bed together that night, but I knew the notion had not occurred to her, and I was not about to suffer a humiliating rejection.

CHAPTER TWENTY - AN INVITATION I SHOULD HAVE REFUSED

The following day, the topic of Richard and the diamonds came up. Caroline had spoken to a friend who knew Richard well to see if she had any news about him. Keen to conceal her whereabouts from her, she told her she was in the USA. It transpired that Richard had been shot outside a bar in Harare and died of his wounds in hospital. This revelation had no effect on her. I was surprised by her lack of emotion, but this was not Eleanor. From what she said, she suffered no guilt in taking the diamonds from his bedroom. She believed she had done the right thing. Perhaps her actions eventually led to his death? It was not my place to proffer such a possibility.

This confirmed what I already knew about Caroline. She was a tough character, almost devoid of emotion. It was clear she had a challenging life and those experiences shape personalities. I cannot deny I was attracted to her, but in a different way to Eleanor.

She had been staying with me for several days now and I was still asking myself the same question. *Why me? Why had she made contact?* I needed to know, to be satisfied that she had indeed only called on a whim, so I asked her.

She had thought long and hard about making contact, wanting closure on Eleanor's death. She needed to discover the truth, to satisfy her mind that she knew all the facts so she could move on with her life. Her feelings for me prior to Eleanor's death had clouded her thinking. It was easy to assume that this callous man who had robbed her of her sister's affection during her childhood had murdered her, but she knew she needed more facts. There had been no doubt in her mind that I had committed the crime, because a jury had found me guilty, but even to her, the evidence seemed slim at the time. As the years passed, she had become less emotional and more analytical, finally arriving at the decision that I was more than likely innocent.

I was grateful that I now knew her motive for the visit. I thanked her for being candid.

She asked if she could stay one more night and leave for London the following morning. Of course, I agreed. After supper, she insisted on sleeping together. It was a bizarre turnaround. A few days earlier I had been tempted to ask her to share my bed, but now it did not seem right. I was attracted to her, but it seemed out of character for her to suggest such a thing. My reaction must have seemed odd. Most single men, when faced with such a request from a beautiful woman, would jump at the chance without hesitation. Instead, I asked her if she had thought it through. Was it wise to complicate an already complicated situation? She laughed! *She could not remember the last time a man had refused her.* It was odd. I was the one concerned about the awkwardness of sleeping together, not her. Why would she want to sleep with a man that had gone to bed with her sister and possibly murdered her? We went to bed. It was an extraordinary experience.

When we got up, to my disappointment, Caroline was not as affectionate as I hoped she would be. I put it down to her personality. I made breakfast and raised the subject of her leaving for London. She was planning a late morning train. Out of the blue, she asked if I would accompany her to Harare in a week's time as she wanted to recover the diamonds. The invitation took me by surprise. Seeing as she would be in Zimbabwe, she thought it would be a good idea to travel across to South Africa for a break for a few days. I was thrilled she had asked me. Perhaps a relationship was on the cards. It was more than I had expected a few days earlier, although the prospect of a serious relationship seemed in some way disloyal to Eleanor. I wonder what she would have thought about it.

Caroline boarded the late morning train and said she would make all the arrangements for the trip and would be in touch. As I walked back through town, I was in a quandary. I felt distinctly uneasy and tried to fathom why. I took account of the fact that Caroline's persona was different from Eleanor's. I could not expect to draw any comparisons. I had already deduced that Caroline was more analytical and less emotional than Eleanor. She was a cool character, measured and less tactile. I was attracted to her, but a relationship with her would be on different terms, her terms. Accepting that rationale, I still felt uncomfortable. There was something not quite right. Perhaps it was because I knew how upset she had been with me when, according to her, I stole Eleanor from her. She was bitter to the core and despite my attempting all those years ago to patch things up she was adamant that I was the enemy. So, what had changed? Was it just the passing of time? I was imprisoned for killing her sister. Even if she believed I was innocent, and I was not convinced she thought I was, it would be a huge chasm to cross to embrace me - even more, to sleep with me. Caroline was a measured woman. She had to have an agenda, but what was it?

I got back to the cottage. She had left some of her new clothes behind. I picked up a sweater and imagined her wearing it. It was as though I wanted her clothing to tell me about her intentions. What was she thinking? It was impossible to think of anything else for the rest of the day. I had committed to going to Africa with her, and in many respects, I was looking forward to the break, but something told me I should abandon the idea and get on with my uncomplicated life in Winchester, where I was beginning to settle into a new normality. Caroline after all represented the past, and the past often clings to you. How could I ever really forget about the awful events on Boxing Day, when I had discovered Eleanor dead, if Caroline were in my life? I would be constantly haunted by her presence.

Two days later, Caroline sent me an email, detailing our travel plans.

CHAPTER TWENTY-ONE - THE

TRIP TO AFRICA

In planning the itinerary, she said she wanted to try and sell the diamonds in Harare or in Cape Town before returning. However, she knew she would get a better price in London and was undecided on what to do. From Caroline's estimate, the bag contained over fifty large diamonds, potentially worth more than a half a million pounds sterling.

Who really owned the diamonds? It was impossible to determine; Richard was dead. If he had lawfully owned them, his sister, Abigail - Caroline's friend - could lay claim to them if she knew anything about them. Caroline believed it would be too difficult to prove their provenance without a long and thorough investigation. She decided *we* would share the proceeds once they were sold. When she announced this on the 'phone, I felt distinctly uncomfortable. Why should I share in the booty? It was a nice gesture, but it seemed unfitting that I should. I still had serious reservations about making the trip in the first place and this revelation made me feel even more uncomfortable. In hindsight, I should have declined the invitation to travel with her at this point, but I agreed to go.

Caroline had a trusted friend, Laura Janson, who had recently married Neville DeVries, an older man who had successfully run a fashion business in South Africa before selling up. They lived in Johannesburg. He was well connected and had always liked Caroline. It was a long shot, but she thought it might be worth having a confidential meeting with him to see if he knew of anyone that might be interested in buying the diamonds without asking too many questions. The idea sounded dubious, but it was not my call. Caroline called Laura and managed to speak to Neville. He was confident that he could help. Caroline would plan everything, arranging to meet in Johannesburg.

I opened the email and read through the itinerary. We would be away for seven days. On day one, we would travel from London Heathrow to Harare, a thirteen-hour flight. There was only a two-hour time difference, which made it easier to adjust upon arrival. We would pick up the bag of diamonds from the safety deposit box. From there, we would check in to an airport hotel and stay in Harare the following day. On day three, she would hire a car that would take us on a five-and-a-half -hour drive to Bulawayo, to see a friend she had promised to visit. We would check in to a local hotel for the night. On day four, we would drop the hire car off at the airport and fly from Bulawayo to Johannesburg to meet with Neville and his contact, hopefully to sell the diamonds. We would stay over at the Tower Hotel and fly out to Cape Town on day five, where we would stay for two days, relaxing. Finally, on day seven, we would return to London.

It all started exactly as she had described. We left Heathrow on a Sunday morning, heading for Harare. Caroline had booked business class seats. It was likely to be a grueling week of travel and she wanted to avoid fatigue. We slept most of the journey. It was a good flight and we arrived on time. After collecting our luggage and travelling through customs, Caroline asked if I would collect the diamonds from the safety deposit box and handed me the key. I did as she asked. She had arranged for someone to pick us up and take us to the hotel. A black Mercedes drew up on the concourse and the driver remained in his seat. He made no effort to assist us with our luggage. Caroline acknowledged him through the window. We stored our bags in the trunk and got into the back seats. Then, we sped away.

I remembered the hotel Caroline had arranged for us was in the vicinity of the airport. The driver said nothing to either of us the whole time; he was just doing his job. I looked into Caroline's eyes and smiled but there was no emotion, she was expressionless. I went to hold her hand, but she pulled away and looked at me as though I repulsed her. Quietly, I asked if she was okay, but she ignored me and looked straight ahead. I glanced up at the rearview mirror and caught site of the driver's eyes and cheekbones. His face seemed familiar, but I was unable to place him. We gained pace and by now, we had left the airport long behind us. I sensed something was very wrong.

We pulled over at speed into a deserted industrial area and stopped sharply. Before I had a chance to ask any questions, both Caroline and the driver got out. He strode round to the back door where I was sitting, and opened it, dragging me to the ground. It was Eleanor's brother - Caroline's brother, David. The first time I had seen him in decades. He punched me in the face, tied my hands behind me, and put a gag in my mouth. Before he had an opportunity to blindfold me, I looked directly at Caroline to see if I could discover anything in her expression. She took one look at me and spat in my face. Blindfold on, he dragged me to another stationary car that I had seen as we arrived. He opened the trunk and manhandled me in. The lid slammed shut. I heard David. "No. I'll take him. You drive the Mercedes back to the airport and I'll see you tomorrow". I failed to hear a response from Caroline. The engine started and we drove away at speed. To say I was confused would be an understatement. I simply could not comprehend what was happening to me. My face was so sore that I wondered if my jaw had been broken. I was being thrown from one side of the car to the other. There was no point in shouting out; who would be there to hear me?

I estimated the journey took twenty minutes before the car drew to a halt. I felt physically sick. David got out, slammed the car door, and opened the trunk. He grabbed me by the collar of my jacket and hauled me out. I dropped to the ground without struggling. It was futile. He dragged me some way before he let me fall to the ground again. I lay there, breathing hard. I heard him open a door. He picked me up and forced me inside, pushing me a few feet into another room, where I plunged to the floor. "So, you thought you'd got away with it, you bastard!" He kicked me twice in the ribs, and again in the head. Then, he slammed the door and left.

I lay there, motionless. It was too painful to move. I could feel myself losing consciousness, but I fought hard to stay awake. Under the circumstances, I was incredibly calm, although I was struggling to breath. The conditions were perfect to have a panic attack. I was choking. I knew I had to maintain my composure if I were to stay alive; whether that was the best option I was unsure. David's parting remark told me all I needed to know. Caroline's visit to Winchester, the sex, and the invitation to travel with her to Harare were all a ploy to lure me in. It was as plain as daylight. My serving 12 years in prison for murdering Eleanor was not enough for them. They wanted me dead and as the UK custodial system had failed do it for them, they would reap their own revenge. I reflected on my time with Caroline and all the signs were there. She was cold and aloof. She was calculating. But why the invitation to have sex? I would have thought that would be the last thing on her mind when you consider how much she despised me, detested me. Perhaps it was a perverse act, the desire to have something that her sister had had before her. Who knows? The irony, of course, was that I did not murder Eleanor. Their barbarism was misplaced, but that was of no consequence now. It was clear, irrespective of their hatred for me, that these were exceptional lengths to go to get me out of the country to kill me. The catalogue of lies Caroline had told me when describing her story at the cottage, which I had believed, was worthy of a booker prize. Why bother? Why not pay a hitman to dispose of me in Winchester without having to knock on my door? There were so many questions running through my mind, but few answers. In a strange way, I was pleased I was not lying there waiting to die without knowing the reason why. I knew. I had killed their sister, or at least they believed I had, and as the saying goes, 'An eye for an eye'.

The adrenalin pumping around my body was wearing off and my calmness was turning to panic. I was struggling for breath and I knew I had to get my heart rate down or I would be dead by morning.

David had tied my hands so tightly that blood was a rare commodity in my wrists and the pain was excruciating. I thought about the movies, in which people regularly escape from being tied up. This was not possible in my case. The blindfold had slipped, albeit only slightly and I had some limited vision. The gag was choking me. A light was on in the next room. The room I occupied was quite small and paint was flaking off the walls. A lightbulb hung from the ceiling. There were items stacked in one corner, although I was unable to determine what they were. I was lying on my side I had no choice my hands were tied behind me. I was able to move my legs, but every movement was difficult. I was sure David had broken my ribs as well as my jaw. Every breath caused pain. The reality of my plight was not lost on me. I knew I was going to die. What was not clear, was when and how that final act would be perpetrated.

I kept as still as I could to avoid further discomfort and save energy. I was tired and the pain I was experiencing now radiated from every part of my body. I knew if I fell asleep, it might be my last. I also knew that to die now, to die this very night, might well be the best I could hope for. I was resigned to my fate. There was no doubt in my mind that they absolutely, unequivocally, believed I was guilty of Eleanor's murder. Of course, there are countless thousands of family members who see loved ones murdered, and while they may have thoughts of revenge, they rarely go to the lengths Caroline and David had to entrap their prey.

I drifted back in time. I was sitting in the Villiers Street restaurant. Staring out of the window. I saw the most beautiful woman dressed in a long black coat. The coat had a brown fur collar, and she wore a red hat and lipstick to match. It was pouring with rain and she looked incredibly sad, as though she were standing at the graveside of a loved one. I wondered who she was and whether I would...I had only fifteen minutes to get to the station to catch a train to the west country...He was tall and slim he put his kit bag... ...I heard a gunshot, and he was... The license plates were Polish...I looked but... ...My eyes shut. I drifted off.

As I regained consciousness. I had no idea how long I had been out, but I was very weak. I drifted in and out of thoughts that made no sense. I knew that moving about caused pain, so I was resigned to staying perfectly still. Dehydration was a big factor facing me. I needed water but I had to put that out of my mind. My mask had slipped completely and was now resting on my nose. I could see everything, albeit there was little to see. The room was windowless, so the only light I had was from the room next door. I sensed the building was a shed of some sorts. It reminded me of being at the allotments with Peter. We were sitting in the potting shed as the light from the paraffin lamp bounced around the room. It was cold and we shivered. Now, it was far too hot, and I was sweating. I was in Harare, Zimbabwe, a world away from my reality. Here, the justice system was brutal and unforgiving, not that I was on trial. I had already been sentenced to death. No one was out there fighting my corner. I had no lawyer to defend me. The truth is that I was alone, at the mercy of Caroline and David, and they could dispense whatever punishment they saw fit for a murderer.

The mind plays games at times like this. I tried to imagine what would have happened if Caroline's invitation to travel with her had been sincere.

CHAPTER TWENTY-TWO -

REPRIEVE

I had been lying on my side for almost a day. I had no feelings in my arms and legs. The only thing I could feel was my life slipping away. I knew the end was near. I heard a car draw up outside. The door opened and I heard David and Caroline talking. They came in. It was clear that Caroline was visibly moved by the sight of me. She wondered if I was still alive. David bent down and I saw him looking at me. He took out a knife and cut the wrist ties. I lay still. I could not move even if I wanted to. I raised my eyelids - it was as much as I could do. David sat me up and took the choke out of my mouth. My mouth was parched. It was a hot day, but I was cold and shaking. Caroline went to the car and came back with bottled water and offered it to me. My arms were lifeless. The wrist tie had stopped the flow of blood to my hands and arms and they were unable to function. She held the bottle to my lips and inadvertently poured water down my face. The minute amount I was able to swallow tasted so good. My mouth and throat were raw. I could barely swallow, despite my desperate thirst. They went into the other room. For some minutes as I began to come to, I heard them talking. They were shocked by my condition. They had not anticipated that I would deteriorate so quickly. Of course, I had been kicked and punched, tied up and gagged, and left for dead. I wondered what they had expected. I needed urgent medical attention, but I doubted that was on the cards. They wanted me dead and were clearly close to achieving that objective. So, why come back? Why not just leave me to die and let someone else discover me in weeks, months, or maybe never?

David came back into the room while Caroline waited outside, too squeamish no doubt. I was only just conscious and totally at his mercy. He asked me what I thought they should do with me. I thought the question was moronic, no doubt a bare attempt to justify the torment they had already inflicted upon me. He was keen to remind me that this was all my fault. I had killed their sister, Eleanor, and as the liberal justice system back in the UK had only given me a *holiday* in prison, they had no option but to take the law into their own hands. I had killed her, so I should die too. I listened to his speech and made no attempt to either agree with his thinking or argue my case. I was in no fit state to do so, and even if I had been, it was highly unlikely they would listen to a word I said.

My ears pricked up when David declared that they had no immediate plans to kill me. Instead, they would kill my children if I failed to do what they had in mind for me. The very mention of my children stirred great emotion in my being. I tried to speak, although I had no voice. Another revelation came to his lips that stunned me. I had seen photos in Eleanor's house that Christmas of her, Mike, and their daughter Charlotte on the yacht. The photo had been taken a year prior to the sailing accident when Mike and Charlotte had drowned. According to David, I was Charlotte's father, not Mike. He never knew he was raising another man's child. According to Caroline, Eleanor had never told him. I remembered examining the photo when Eleanor took Barney for a walk, casually thinking she had some of my features. She was beautiful, like Eleanor. This news served to rub increasing amounts of salt into the gaping wound that was my life. I had helped bring a child into the world but had had no hand in raising her. As David went on, often raising his voice, I could only think of the years I had lost. What had she been like? Her moods, her temperament, her charm, her personality, before her drowning?

I became so absorbed in these thoughts that I failed to hear a word of what David was saying. The only two things that resonated in my ears were my children and the threat to their lives, and Charlotte and a life I would never know. He kicked me to wake me out of the trance I was in. I felt no pain. I was incapable of feeling anything, either mentally or physically. I was helpless. Before he left, he chained me to a metal pulley in the corner of the room, locked the outside door, and left. The car sped off. I was alone again.

About an hour passed when a car pulled up. This time, Caroline was on her own. She brought food and a first aid kit. By now, I was able to get to my knees but no more. At first, Caroline said nothing. She just tried to feed me. I was hungry but I had little appetite. Occasionally, I would look up at her to try and discern her mood, to see if there was any guilt in her eyes for what they were doing to me or had planned for me. I resisted saying anything at first, then I managed to eke out a sentence. "Why, Caroline? Why are you doing this to me?" She chose to remain silent. She undid the chain, took my jacket and shirt off, and saw the injury David had inflicted upon me. My face was raw, and it hurt when I moved my face. Again, I wondered if my jaw had been broken. She patched me up as best she could, I took a few sips from the water bottle before she put the chain back on. I had missed an opportunity to escape when the chains were removed, but the truth is I did not have the strength to do anything about it. Caroline could easily have overpowered me.

She chose this moment to say something. "You knew how close I was to Eleanor when we were children and later, when you had the affair, but you just didn't care. Eleanor and I were inseparable until you came along and then my life came to an end when you murdered her". Of course, she did not believe my Oscar-winning performance back in Winchester. Her tone was not aggressive - it was heart-felt. I sensed she was not about to plunge a dagger in my heart, so what I said next would be crucial if I had any chance of bringing this drama to an end – or at least, one in which I remained alive. My voice was croaky, so I took my time. "I know anything I say to you will appear desperate. I know my life hangs by a thread. I am not fearful of what you and David might do to me. After all, I can do little to stop you. My fear is for my children. I hope what David said earlier was an idle threat and you are not serious about harming them. They should not be expected to pay for anything you believe I have done. I know I have hurt you beyond imagination, and I know you will never believe me, but as God looks over me, and my children's lives, I did *not* kill Eleanor".

Her facial expression changed. She had tears in her eyes. I had no way of knowing, but I hoped that the time she had spent with me in Winchester would lead her to believe that I was not capable of murder, let alone the murder of Eleanor. She showed no signs of affection for me over those few days, but she had slept with me. I quickly discounted that encounter, but it may have been a factor.

She listened without interruption. It was too much for her to deal with. I could see the cogs in her mind, churning. Finally, she said, "You have water and some food. That will last you until we return". With that, she closed and locked the front door and drove off.

My physical condition had changed little but my mind was more positive. I thought that I may, just may have got through to Caroline. I would find out in good time. It had not occurred to them, but it was certainly occurring to me, that the various calls of nature were reminding me I was human. I wondered how I would be able to contain my bodily requirements until they returned. I hoped they would return soon.

I tugged at the chain, albeit gently. I had no energy. If my strength returned, it would not be difficult to free myself. I held that thought in mind. I wondered what Caroline and David were doing now. Were they regretting their abduction and thinking of a way of bringing it to an end, preferably without having to kill me? Or were they intent upon somehow using me with the threat that my children would be harmed if I failed to comply? I had no way of knowing, but for some strange reason, I was positive of mind.

It had been some hours since Caroline left. I had fallen asleep and when I awoke, I was almost unable to move. I needed exercise but first, I needed the bathroom.

I heard the familiar sound of the car approaching. Instead of screeching to a halt, though, it drew up quite slowly. Perhaps it was a positive sign that they were less agitated. I was clutching at straws. They both entered the room. David showed no signs of aggression. Before they had a chance to say anything, I asked to visit the bathroom. It was a polite term under the circumstances, but they got the message. David unchained me and helped me to walk outside. The sun pierced my eyes. I was so weak he had to drag me around the back of the building. It was a roadside fruit and veg shack that was long deserted. Perhaps trade dried up or the demand to house captives had become less fashionable? The thought amused me, and I chuckled. David looked at me as though I had lost my mind. Perhaps I had. He left me to do my business; there was little chance of me running off.

I returned of my own volition. They were talking. I could hear them disagreeing about something, probably what to do next. I asked if I could remain standing and they agreed. I propped myself up against a wall and listened to what they had to say. David spoke. His tone was firm but less threatening. He remained assertive. Caroline just looked at me. This time, she was not about to spit in my face. I sensed I had won her over.

"I want you to know, nothing has changed. Your little chat with Caroline failed. She told me what you said. I certainly don't believe you!" His comment suggested that Caroline did believe me. That, I hoped, was good news. If I had one of them on my side, I was making progress. "We're taking you to a house for a few days so you can recover your strength and then I have a few jobs for you". I was eager to find out. "What kind of jobs?" I asked. Although I had only uttered those few words, I could see David was not about to indulge me in dialogue. "You'll find out." With that, Caroline assisted me, a little too strongly, I felt pain rush down my arm, but it was good that she was making the effort rather than David.

David put the blindfold back on me. We drove off in silence and it remained that way for the rest of the journey. Half an hour later, we arrived at our destination and this time Caroline removed the blindfold. I was under strict instructions to stay silent and move as quickly as I could. It was a small condominium. We walked down a short path to the front door and entered. I was guided into the sitting room. It was sparsely furnished but quite adequate. I doubt anyone lived there permanently.

I thought it unlikely that they would leave me there alone. I hoped if one of them stayed, it would be Caroline. David left and said he would be back in the morning. Before he did, I was told I would not be chained up, but that if I tried to escape or did anything to Caroline, my children would die. It was probably an idle threat, but I was not about to test his resolve. I could see how awkward this was for Caroline. Irrespective of whether she now believed I was innocent of Eleanor's murder or not, her attitude toward me had changed for the better. I thought it wrong to make assumptions that I could start a friendly conversation with her; after all, I had been abducted, beaten, and held hostage.

She offered to make some tea. I was still dehydrated, and tea sounded wonderful, unimaginable considering that a few hours earlier, I had been speculating if they would abandon me to a certain death.

She came back with the tea and handed me a mug. I expected her to leave the room straight away, but she stayed. She sat on the sofa as I gradually lowered myself onto a chair. I was no longer crippled but I was still in some considerable pain. My breathing had improved, and my chest was less sore, I could only conclude that my ribs were intact. There was a brief silence then Caroline started to talk. "I know all this was a mistake, Lawrence. I shouldn't have agreed to abduct you." I tried to respond immediately, not quite knowing what I was about to say, but she shut me down. "I don't want you to say anything. Nothing you can say will bring my sister back." She was right, repeating my story again was pointless. "David cannot forgive you. He believes with his heart that you murdered Eleanor and nothing you can say will change his mind. I would advise you not to try. He knows that it was a mistake to bring you out to Harare. When he returns tomorrow, he will ask you to do several things, and I want you to agree to do whatever he asks." I remained silent. Perhaps I was reading too much into her words, but it seemed as though she was genuinely keen to protect my welfare. Perhaps she even cared what happened to me. I hoped so. I nodded in the affirmative.

She suggested I went to bed to sleep. I was reminded of the bath I took at the roadside café after drudging through the woodlands, caked in mud. The feeling of the hot water flowing over me was a dream come true. I looked forward to bed in the same way and hoped my dream of bringing this saga to a close in the morning would be a reality.

I slept solidly and woke early, as I always did. The sun was rising and, along with it, the temperature. I took the liberty of taking a cool shower. By the time I came out of the bathroom, Caroline was making tea. I wanted to greet her like a lover or long-lost friend, but though the better of it. She acknowledged my presence and offered to make breakfast. My appetite had returned. We sat outside on the verandah and I wondered if it stirred any memories of doing so on her grandfather's farm. She looked pensive and distant again. "Does this remind you of your grandfather's verandah?" A bit clumsy, I thought. "Why, should it? You know nothing about my grandfather." Of course, she was wrong. She had told me back in Winchester in some detail about the times she had spent there, and the wonderful memories of the lunches and cakes her grandmother made. I assumed her stories were true. "Don't you remember telling me about your childhood?" She remained silent, got up and went back into the kitchen. I assumed I had hit a raw nerve.

Within the hour, David had arrived. I could see he had come well-rehearsed. I was about to discover what he had in mind for me. From Caroline's tone the day before, my tasks would not be easy, but I had given her the reassurance that I would conform to whatever he demanded of me. I was resigned to doing his bidding.

I sat in the chair I adopted the previous evening and he sat on the sofa. Caroline was upstairs. "For the next week or so, you'll be doing a lot of travelling. I have a business and you will work for me. I will, and I repeat, *will*, kill your children if you fail to do what I say. Is that understood?" He looked at me with that thuggish expression I had seen so many times in prison. The look of a bully. The look that says, 'I'm in control, cross me and you're dead'. In this instance, it was my children that were the target, the value of their lives far outweighing my own. Of course, I would do what he ordered me to do. "I understand." I would not beg or plead with him; that was futile, counter-productive! No. I would indulge him when, where, and how he wanted me to, but I needed to know when my penance would be served. When I would be off the hook and able to get back to some sort of life? When would I know my children were safe?

I braced myself and thought about the words I was about to utter very carefully. "David, I will do as you ask. My children are all important to me. Can you assure me that once I have completed what you have planned that they will be safe? He looked at me in an unkindly way, as I was expecting. "Like it or not, you *will* do what I say. I'll tell you if I think you've paid the price for murdering my sister." The words were not comforting. The price of his sister's life surely had more value to him than a weeks' work. I sensed that I might never be free of him for as long as I lived. In his eyes, she died because of me. So, I will die because of him. I asked to be excused.

I slowly made my way up the stairs to the bathroom. The next phase was discovering precisely what my mission was. I returned to the sitting room. Caroline had come down and was in the kitchen making coffee. I sat down in what had become *my* chair. David sat opposite me and Caroline discreetly made her exit once more.

David presented me with a large envelope. He had chosen to recycle a used one. I approved of that at least. I took out the contents and found an itinerary and a description of my duties. I stole a cursory glance across at David. He looked back at me sternly and encouraged me to study the detail well. My travel would take me to Johannesburg, Cape Town, and London. My duties included the smuggling of diamonds and drugs, as well as the *occasional assassination*! As demanded, I read the details carefully. It was as though I were reading the script of a thriller movie, a James Bond film, but this was not a fantasy thriller you read in a book or watched at the movies before returning to a normal life. This was real. This was what David expected of me, or my children would die. Now, I would be the first to admit that I was not the ideal candidate for the job. This was not my line of expertise. I knew plenty of people far better qualified, who would relish the opportunity to execute his orders back in Belmarsh prison, but fortunately for society, they were unavailable. David knew it would be almost impossible for me to do his dirty work and not die in the process. By recruiting me, he had found the perfect stooge. I would smuggle and kill for his benefit until my luck ran out and I would die, as his sister had done. An eye for eye. It was perfect.

CHAPTER TWENTY-THREE -

THE EXECUTION

E very detail had been carefully and meticulously worked out: the flights I would take, the cars I'd travel in, the hotels I'd stay in, the people I'd meet - and those I was to kill, and how they would meet their demise. He told me that someone would be watching or tracking me all the time and, on occasions, would assist with my assignments. It was all there, as well as knowing that I was to start the day after tomorrow. There was no way I could escape or walk away. This was not a game. He had done his homework. He knew my children's names, where they lived, the names of their mothers. I felt guilt at the thought that they would be embroiled in all this. David had someone watching the house in case I thought I could run away or so he said.

He left after the briefing and said I would receive what I needed, including the clothes Caroline had taken from the cottage without my knowing and packed in her bags for the trip, which I was to discover included Mike's suit and shirt. I would also receive all the relevant documentation, including the return of my passport in the morning. I thought I might be travelling under a false name but why would he go to those lengths? It served no useful purpose. No, if I were caught, it would be me, Christopher Jason, that would be apprehended. It was all part of the plan. There was little time to take it all in.

Caroline came down and we sat in the sitting room. I wondered why people always took up residence in the same chair, but that was precisely what I had done. She asked me what I thought. There was a concerned look on her face as she obviously knew what David had planned for me. It was odd, but I was not fearful of what lay ahead. I was more interested in what Caroline now thought of me. She had only recently been made aware that David was involved in drugs and diamond smuggling. They spent little time together in recent years, she had just assumed he was a successful businessman and never questioned what his specialty was. Now, she knew. He had always been different from Eleanor and Caroline. Growing up, he was quick to assume the dominant role. He got into trouble on a regular basis and was thrown out of public school for taking drugs and wrecking a car. From an early age, he was destined for bad things. Interestingly, David was dyslexic like so many of the prisoners I met in Belmarsh. Was there a connection, I thought? I asked her if she was aware of the contents of the envelope. She said not, and did not want to know, but assumed it had something to do with smuggling. I encouraged her to open the envelope, but she refused. "I don't want to know what you'll be doing, just that you'll do what he asks so that you and the children will be safe." There was a genuine expression of concern on her face. These were encouraging words. Caroline was showing a different side of her personality now. She was different from when we were together in Winchester and different again from when she had spat at me as I was dragged out of the car the previous day. This was her true persona, her caring, nurturing side. I liked it. "I'll do what David asks of me, but how well I will execute his instructions I'm not sure. Thank you. The word *execute* was probably not a wise choice. I looked her in the eyes almost lovingly. I was a sucker for anyone who expressed kindness or their true feelings. I had just witnessed what I thought was a turning point in my relationship with her.

David was not expected back. Without anything further being said, Caroline took my hand and led me upstairs to the bedroom. There, we spent the night together. I was in no fit state to do anything other than hold her gently in my arms. The experience was more than enough for both of us.

I woke early and took the opportunity to study the contents of the envelope once more. My acceptance of David's plan had been somewhat cavalier for a man who was almost certainly destined to die for a cause to which he did not in any way subscribe to. My outward look did not reflect the true feelings running through my fragile mind. I had already been beaten and held captive. Now, as if that were not enough, I faced the reality of playing the pawn in a game of chess I could not win. I was a novice and David, the Grand Master. One ill-considered or naïve move on my part would have serious consequences. Fear ran through my veins. I began to sweat. Was I dreaming all this? Had my mind wandered to another realm, as it had done when I sat there at my trial for Eleanor's murder? At times like this, the mind goes into overdrive. It is impossible to think or act rationally. There was no fear for my own life. If I were to die carrying out David's orders, so be it, but I could not risk the chance that my children might suffer. I had no choice. To see a light at the end of the tunnel I had to toughen up and accept that I was playing a game I *could* win. In my mind, I had to see myself as the Grand Master, and hope that my inner steel would carry me through.

I made tea for Caroline and took it to the bedroom. How many hostages would voluntarily do such a thing for their captive? The thought amused me. Of course, I no longer saw her in that light. It was clear we had created a new bond. I only hoped she had not changed her mind. I put her tea down, leant over and kissed her on the cheek. She opened her eyes and tried to smile but there was anguish in her face. I hoped it was for fear of what might happen to me, but either way, she forced a smile.

It was soon after 9.30am when a car drew up outside. A well-built man who had spent far too much time working out in the gym came to the door with a large brown suitcase, a briefcase, and a box. My first instinct was to let him in, but Caroline stopped me. It would be the clothes and documentation David had told me to expect. Caroline opened the door and the man walked in. He looked me over and smiled. I felt sure that this was his way of letting me know that I had no hope of finishing this task alive. He put the items down and left.

I had twenty-four hours before I would be collected for my first assignment. Caroline looked worried. I opened the suitcase to discover my clothes from the cottage. She had chosen well. "I'm sorry, David. I regret agreeing to be involved in any way with all this. I hope you'll forgive me!" She started to cry. I held her as tightly as I could without breaking my ribs. "I really don't blame you. I can see David is a bully and you had little choice." We spent an hour talking. I left the contents of the suitcase and the box until later. She explained that for years after Eleanor's funeral he had vowed, once I had been released from prison, that he would hunt me down and kill me. She had seen this statement of revenge as a part of the grieving process, never imagining he would carry out his threat. After discovering I had been released, his people track me down. I was followed from Guildford to Winchester. He was building his trafficking business in South Africa at the time and put any ideas for me on hold. Eventually, he arranged a lunch date with Caroline and told her of his plans. She was horrified and begged him not to do anything, to let sleeping dogs lie, but he was adamant that I would properly pay for his sister's murder. He bullied her into agreeing to lure me in. She felt she had no choice, but she insisted that other than getting me to Harare, she didn't know what would be expected of me. I believed her.

I unpacked the suitcase. There were additional clothes that David or one of his cronies had bought for me, presumably believing they would give me a certain look. Among the accessories was a pair of designer sunglasses, the kind mobsters wear to look cool. Everything I needed was there. I also found my passport, airline tickets, and various documents that would add credence to my new role as a murderer-cum-smuggler-cum-drug-trafficker, and everything corresponded to the itinerary that David had handed to me in the recycled envelope the day before.

My first assignment was to travel by car to a warehouse on the outskirts of Harare. A driver would take me there. I was to collect a package and take it to another address the other side of town. From there, I would go to an airport hotel and wait for a flight to Johannesburg the following morning. It seemed easy enough; what was there to worry about?

Having told me the story of her involvement, which I believed, Caroline was now more relaxed around me. It was as though we were the couple in the café at Waterloo station all those years ago who sat opposite each other totally consumed by their emotions, not wanting to part company. That feeling of love, of being consumed by another's presence, was a powerful cocktail that focused the mind to the exclusion of everything else. Caroline knew this may be the last day we spent together, and she wanted to make the most of it. We talked and talked. It was a liberating experience. We got to know almost everything about each other, although we avoided the subject of Eleanor. It was clearly still too raw in her mind. I believed that would always be the case. It was a bizarre and therapeutic exchange at the same time, and it gave me hope that one day, assuming I came out of this alive, we could be together.

Again, I woke early. I was packed and ready to go. We both had a disturbed night's sleep with so much going on in our minds. We clung together throughout the night, not wanting to let the other go. I made tea and toast, then we sat on the verandah and listened to the birds singing as the sun rose bright and big in the sky. It would be a hot and muggy day. Caroline said she was thinking of leaving for London the following day and would not return. I told her to go to the Winchester cottage and wait for me there. It was my way of giving her reassurance that I would get through this ordeal and we would be together afterwards. She sobbed for an hour. I had not seen this side of her. I tried to comfort her as best I could, but she was despairing. This was a ridiculous, misguided vendetta that David was bestowing upon me, but there was no way out, no escape. I was no longer so cavalier about my own life now that I knew I had Caroline's affection, and my heart broke at the thought that I may never see her again.

I sat in my adopted chair and waited for the car to arrive. We had said our goodbyes. Caroline did not want to wait with me; her emotions were running too high. She went up to the bedroom and it all went quiet. Soon enough, the car drew up and there was a knock at the door. I collected the suitcase and briefcase and closed the door behind me. Outside, I looked up at the window and saw the curtain twitching. Caroline wanted a last look at the man who she had despised a few days earlier, but who she now loved – or so I hoped. I followed the driver to a black Mercedes, the same one that had picked us up from the airport. I got into the back and wondered what was in store for me. The driver was dressed in black, wearing the customary gangster shades. He looked straight ahead and delivered a well-rehearsed speech. Did I know where I was going? Did I understand what I had to do? I responded in the affirmative. He would take me to the warehouse and wait for me in the car. The traffic was heavy. We made slow progress. My hands were sweating, and I was breathing heavily. I had to remind myself that I was doing this for my children, and I needed to adopt an air of confidence and think clearly if I were to succeed. We arrived on the outskirts of Harare and pulled into a small, rundown estate. The buildings were in a poor state of repair and there was nobody around. The driver looked in the rearview mirror, dropped his glasses down his nose so I could see his eyes, and nodded. That was my sign to get out of the car and enter the building. I was expected.

I took a deep breath and tried to maintain my composure. I was still in pain from David's beating and walked with a limp. I entered a side door and was confronted by a burly man standing in front of me. There was no conversation. No "hello, how are you?" This was the world I had got to know in prison. You spoke when you were spoken to. You smiled when you wanted to humiliate someone, not because you were expressing warmth and affection. I was led into a scruffy office. The man behind a desk was on the 'phone and was clearly not pleased. He was berating someone for not doing something or other. I had no interest one way or the other. He stared at me throughout the conversation. I averted my attention. I had discovered in prison that it was necessary to do so if you were to avoid confrontation. Staring at someone was defiant and provocative. I was there to pick something up, not get into a fight or, worse still, a shooting match. He put the receiver down.

"So, a new boy, are you? Got you doing his dirty work?" I stayed silent. He leant to one side and picked up a package, a large jiffy bag, which he handed to me. "Can you give me a receipt, boy?" I told him I did not have one. He laughed. "I can see you're new to this game. Watch out for yourself. Whatever deal David's got you on, you are not being paid enough. Dangerous work, my friend!" Little did he know, my pay was non-existent. My reward was my children's lives. I took the package from him and was led back out to the car. I got in and breathed a sigh of relief. My driver once again dropped his glasses onto his nose and looked in the rearview mirror. This time, he smiled. "Any problems?" I said nothing but nodded to suggest the transaction had gone well. We drove across town again. The traffic had eased. Arriving at a busy car park, he drove to the southeastern corner and parked next to a BMW. Two men got out. I opened the door and walked over to them with the package. Without a word, they took it from me, got into the car, and drove off. I returned to the Mercedes and we, too, drove off in the direction of the hotel where I would spend the night. My first assignment had been accomplished. I hoped the rest of my tasks would be that easy, but I had a feeling that might not be the case.

I was dropped off at the hotel and told to be in the lobby at 8.00 am the following morning. I was due to fly to Johannesburg. Upon arrival I would be met by another driver.

I checked in. David had booked me the cheapest room he could find. Why would he do differently? After all, he was not trying to impress me! At least it had a bath. I wanted to call Caroline. I was missing her, but I didn't have a 'phone, nor did I have her number to call. I was alone with my thoughts for the next sixteen hours. I was under strict instructions not to leave the hotel. I was being watched. I wondered if David had really gone to the lengths of having me watched or followed. With my children's safety in jeopardy, if I failed to execute his orders, why would he need to? I also pondered if he really would harm the children or whether this, too, was an idle threat. I was not to know so it was futile to speculate. I had to work on the assumption that he would carry out his threat come what may.

It was a glorious bath. The food in the restaurant was good too. I watched some TV in the hotel lounge before going to bed. I was not ready to sleep but there was little else to do other than to speculate on my future, assuming I had one.

It was the longest night I could ever recall. It seemed I had been awake all night. The room was too hot, and the window was sealed shut. I lay there, sweating.

Before I went down for an early breakfast, I read the itinerary and the instructions I was given. I had studied them a thousand times already, but they failed to register. Most of the assignments were detailed, but not today. All I knew was that my driver would take me to the airport, and I would board a plane for Johannesburg. I would be met at the airport. My driver would hold a sign up with my name on it. He would take me to an unknown destination, at least to me, and hand me my instructions.

I had a good breakfast. I was unsure when I'd eat again, so I made the most of it. At precisely 8.00 am, my driver from the previous day picked me up and took me to the terminal two miles away. He said nothing during the journey. The airport was quite busy. My flight was due in forty minutes, it was a short hop - just under two hours. The flight was full, it being a popular commuter route. Most of those on board were businessmen and women, smartly dressed, no doubt preparing for their upcoming meetings as they tapped on their laptops, iPhones, and tablets. They stared blankly at their screens completely oblivious of those around them and certainly unaware of me and the business I was due to carry out.

I remained quite calm until the plane started to descend and I became anxious. We landed bumpily and made our way to the terminal. I scanned the concourse for my name and found it on a hastily written sign at the back of the waiting crowd. The man holding the sign wore black slacks, a checked shirt, and the mandatory eyewear. He, too, was well built, and it looked as though his face had been re-arranged slightly, presumably from physical encounters whilst *earning his living*.

I set my eyes upon him and he noticed me instantly. There was no welcome, no smile; he simply lowered the name card and walked toward the exit. I followed. The car was parked illegally outside. What else should I have expected? It was another black Mercedes, a popular brand in this type of business, I thought. I got into the back. We drove away from the airport perimeter and stopped in a layby. He took off his sunglasses and turned to face me. He handed me an envelope. This time, it appeared to be an unused one. I opened it. He asked me to read the instructions very, very carefully and not to say a word until I fully understood what I had been ordered to do. Delicately, I unfolded the sheet of paper, turned it over and started to read.

You will be taken to a large supermarket. It will be busy. Your driver will park around the corner. He will hand you a loaded pistol, which you'll put in your pocket. You will enter the supermarket and ask an assistant at the till to see the manager, Pieter Brammer. When he comes across, you will take out the pistol and shoot him twice in the heart. You will immediately return to the car. If you are told he is unavailable, you will go to his office and you will shoot him there. Do not return to the car until you have shot him.

I swallowed hard. I needed to assimilate the instructions. I was to be handed a loaded pistol and ordered to shoot dead a man. Was he a family man just trying to earn a living? Was he innocent or guilty? None of this was my business. I had never held a pistol before, loaded or unloaded, and I had certainly never killed anyone. Of course, I had been convicted and served twelve years for murdering Eleanor, so perhaps that qualified me for the job. In the next minute that followed, I went through a catalogue of emotions. My driver could see the dilemma I faced. He had probably murdered dozens of people in his lifetime, to the point at which lifting a pistol and shooting someone dead was considered nothing more than part of his daily exercise. I, however, was in no way prepared for this. No way could I reconcile murdering someone in cold blood in front of a crowded supermarket full of shoppers going about their business. Killing anyone was abhorrent. Was this really, what David expected of me? He was clearly a smart and ruthless man. He knew that asking me to do this was sweet revenge for killing his sister. But why did I have to kill a random person that probably meant nothing to him? Why not just shoot me and be done with it? No. He wanted me to suffer and this was an inspired way to do it. I looked up at my driver. The only thing he could possibly have seen in my eyes was fear. He handed me the pistol. It was heavier than I imaged. In a deep voice, he said, "Do you know how to use it?" For a moment, I hoped that by saying no, he would volunteer to do it for me. But that was not why he was there. "No. I've never shot a pistol. I've never murdered anyone." He laughed. This was funny to him. He was probably thinking *'You've never killed anyone?! Why not?'* I knew scores of people in Belmarsh, just like him. "Are you going to do it or not? Shall I 'phone the boss?" Of course, he meant David. I asked him if he knew Mr. Brammer. "Sure, he's a louse. Refuses to cough up. It's his turn," he said. By the eloquence of his response, I worked out that Mr. Brammer owed David money, or perhaps he had been offered 'security services' but refused to pay for them. I knew, not. More to the point, I did not want to know. If I got out of the car and ran away, the driver would probably shoot me dead without hesitation. If I got out of the car and shot him myself, I would be murdering a man in cold blood. One way or another, someone was going to die.

The absurdity and futility of the situation was not lost on me, nor was the gravity of the plight I found myself in. I could not take the risk of failing this task. So, I just looked at my driver and nodded. I put the pistol in my pocket and got out of the car. I felt sick and light-headed as the reality of what was about to happen started to dawn on me. I walked to the front of the supermarket and found that it was busy, as I had been told it would be. The automatic doors opened, and I felt the chill of an effective air conditioning system. My mind took me back to the hotel and the sweaty night I had endured. I walked up to the counter and asked for Mr. Brammer. The till assistant pointed in his direction. He was twenty feet away from me. He was average height, balding, middle-aged. He was dressed smartly in a clean, white uniform. I said nothing as he turned to face me. Before I pulled out the pistol, I had a vision of blood spurting from his chest, his shirt turning bright red as it mopped up the residue. His eyes bulged as he dropped to the floor, dead. Soothing music played in the background. It was designed to lure people in and relax them into a soporific state so they would be encouraged to impulse buy. I had never heard rock music in supermarkets and that was why: it would encourage people to rush their shopping and reduce the money going through the tills.

At the very moment I pulled the pistol from my trouser pocket, an announcement came over the audio system: *'Would Mr. Brammer please come to till three?'* Little did he know that this was an invitation to his own death. I pulled the trigger back - it was harder than I thought it would be. Momentarily, I looked down at the pistol as Mr. Brammer, sensing what I was about to do, shoved me backward. He was too late, at least partially. The trigger engaged and a shot fired, hitting him in the leg. He dropped to the floor, howling like a dog. I had to put him out of his misery. I aimed at his heart and fired again. Instantly, he stopped moving, save his right hand, which started to shake uncontrollably. All around me, there was mayhem. People ran about screaming. I stood perfectly still, staring at this carcass before me. One minute, he was going about his business, helping his customers, motivating his team, and earning a living to support his family. The next, he was gone, dead in an instant. I had killed him. The words reverberated through my head. A few seconds later, I came out of my trance and ran to the exit. No one was prepared to take me on, including the security guard, who cleared a path for me to leave as quickly as possible. I got back to the car spattered in blood, pistol in hand. We sped away, tires squealing. I slumped back into my seat and my body collapsed. I threw the pistol on the floor. I looked in the rearview mirror and saw the expression on my driver's face. He was laughing.

How could anyone, no matter how deranged, find murder amusing? I lurched forward and vomited profusely. His reaction to that was far less smiley. He stopped the car as quickly as he could, dragged me out of the back seat, and punched me hard in the stomach. Then, he threw me back into the car, shouting obscenities at me all the while. His language was not worth repeating. It was evident that soiling his car was far more of a crime than shooting a man dead. I did not remember the journey to the hotel. When we arrived, he unceremoniously pulled me out of the car and thrust another envelope into my chest, which dropped to the floor. He also handed me a small cardboard box. I picked up the envelope and staggered into the lobby, dazed. I sat there for some minutes, unable to comprehend what I had done. Crimes of this nature were not uncommon the world over, but they were for me. I checked into my room and lay on the bed, shaking. For once, I hoped I would have a panic attack and die in the most excruciating manner. I deserved it. I kept seeing Mr. Brammer drop to the floor, the blood spurting everywhere. I looked at the shirt I was wearing and a part of him was represented in blood spots spread across my chest. I had the DNA of this dead man there on my shirt to remind me of his death. The shirt could easily be washed, and no one would know, but it was impossible to wash my mind of this abhorrent act. It would be indelibly printed on my mind for as long as I drew breath.

I opened the envelope, dreading what I would discover about my next assignment. I had approximately two hours before I would be picked up again. My day's work was not done. I quickly took off my shirt and the rest of my clothing and threw everything on the floor in a heap. I stood there naked, innocent as the day I was born, but I was certainly no innocent anymore. The word *murderer* had haunted me for years, now I was one. I was no better than all those inmates in Belmarsh who really had taken people's lives, probably for no reason, just like me. I opened the suitcase and grabbed a new set of clothes. Inside, I discovered a mobile phone and a message from Caroline. She had programmed her number into the address book, and left instructions that I was to ring her when it was safe to do so. I dropped back on the bed and fell into a deep sleep clutching the 'phone.

CHAPTER TWENTY-FOUR -

DIAMONDS

I woke with a start. I had thirty-five minutes to read the contents of the envelope fully, open the box, shower, get dressed, and be ready in the lobby for my driver. By now, the supermarket surveillance system must have offered up my picture as I ran from the killing. The likelihood was that the police would be on the lookout, so I knew I needed to be vigilant. Of course, David had thought of that. He was not about to let me get caught, at least not yet. There would be no fun for him if I were unable to complete my tasks. In the box was a wig. I had a beard that was going grey and my hair was thinning. The wig matched my own hair color - whether this was a coincidence or not, I was not to know. I pulled the wig out and was surprised to find that it was quite heavy. I held it up and turned it over. Stitched to both sides was a strip of material, concealing what I could only assume were diamonds. In the roof of the wig was a plastic bag full of a white substance that I guessed was cocaine. I went into the bathroom and tried it on. It fitted perfectly and looked real. Despite the added weight, it was quite comfortable. It was the perfect ruse for a smuggler.

I was exhausted. I was still recovering from the ordeal. Time was marching on. I had to read the instructions in the envelope. *'You will shave off your beard. Dress and wear the wig. Your driver will take you to the airport and give you a return ticket to Cape Town. You will be met at the airport by another driver. He will take you to a location, where you will remove the wig and hand it to your contact. They will remove the contents and hand you back the wig, which you will wear for your return trip to Johannesburg. Someone will meet you at the airport and you will be returned to the hotel.*

So, this time I was a drug and diamond mule. I was not instructed to shoot anyone. I arranged with the hotel to provide me with a razor, scissors, and shaving foam to remove my beard. I had little time to spare. I got the elevator down to the lobby to wait for the driver. The check-in clerk looked quizzically at me as I breezed past the front desk. Was I a paying guest? Had he seen me before? He carried on with his work. I sat near the exit and saw the car arrive. It was the same car and driver as before. I got in and we set off for the terminal. The car had been cleaned - it was spotless. The driver smiled when he saw me in the wig. He knew its purpose. We arrived at the airport. The flight was due in forty minutes. It was just over two hours to get to Cape Town. I felt conspicuous but I went through baggage search without difficulty. I bought a newspaper and sat in the departures lounge. On page four, I saw the headline, *'Supermarket Manager Gunned Down.* It was accompanied by a grainy CCTV picture of me fleeing the scene. I could only assume that being relegated to page four was an indication of how little value society and the media placed on a human life. I put the paper down. I could not contemplate what Mr. Brammer's family and his colleagues were going through. It would haunt them, as it would haunt me for years to come.

My head was itching. I was desperate to scratch it, but for obvious reasons that was difficult in public. I went to the men's room.

Fortunately, there was no one there as I entered. I took the wig off and scratched my head vigorously. Just as I looked in the mirror to put the wig back on, a young man came in and spotted me. It is difficult to say what he thought, but he quickly made his way into a cubicle and remained silent until I left. At least he would have an amusing story to tell his friends later.

You would think I would be anxious about travelling with contraband sitting on and around my head, but I found myself surprisingly relaxed. Nothing could compare to the horror of the day before. If I were stopped and searched, I would have to think on my feet. This was a familiar concept. I went back to the seat I had vacated earlier. The flight was called, and I joined an orderly queue to board. My seat was in the front row, next to the toilet. At least if I needed to scratch again, I could do so without attracting attention. Of the two hundred or so people on the flight, it was the young man in men's room who sat next to me. I could tell that he would rather have sat elsewhere, but it was a full flight. He acknowledged me, but his demeanor suggested he did not want to make idle conversation. That suited me fine. We were silent throughout the flight.

Having landed, I walked through to the concourse. It was an internal flight, so there would be no search at customs. My driver was holding a placard with my name on it. *Christopher Jason.* Of course, it should have been *Lawrence Hogarth,* but like everything else about me, it was a lie or out of character. I was a different man and the name I carried with me was meaningless.

This was becoming a familiar scene. My driver was burly, his arms and neck covered in tattoos. He was short but hugely muscular and wore a perfectly shaped beard, just like the one I had allowed to disappear down the sink back at the hotel. I acknowledged him and again, he just turned and walked toward the exit. No pleasantries. I assumed he had attended the same charm school as my earlier driver. I followed.

We got into a BMW 7 series. At least the brand of car was different. "Nice hair. Your own, is it?" He smiled. He, too, knew the drill. I decided to take the hard mans approached and ignored his remark. There was no envelope with instructions on this occasion. David obviously trusted him to impart what I needed to know. "Right. We have a twenty-minute drive. When we get there, you will get out of the car and go through a door I will point out to you. Inside, ask for Cedric. It will probably be him that will let you in. Take off the wig and wait while he takes out the contents. He will take his time. Once satisfied, he will give you 60,000 rand. Count it in front of him then return to the car. Bring back the wig. Got it?" I had got it. "I'll also give you a loaded pistol. If you think there is anything suspicious inside, anything at all you feel unhappy about shoot him in the head. Do not wait for him to do something to you. Just shoot him. Got it?" I got that too. So, this was how business was transacted. If something was said you chose not to like, you did not raise your concerns verbally, did not negotiate, didn't seek clarification. You simply pulled out a pistol and shot the person opposite you. I could see how this was a regular occurrence in this shady world, and for the psychopaths, addictive, too. It crossed my mind that shooting Cedric might well prove easier for me, mentally at least, than shooting Mr. Brammer. Cedric was a part of the gang culture and had probably killed more people in his career than I could imagine, whereas I suspect Mr. Brammer, like me, had never held a loaded pistol in his life.

We arrived at the back of a row of decrepit shops. The door in front of me was lime green. I was sure that when it had been freshly painted decades ago it had looked attractive, but it had since been allowed to deteriorate and large tracks of paint had flaked away. I was handed a pistol, a smaller, lighter version than the one I used on Mr. Brammer. I slipped it into my pocket, hoping my marksmanship skills would not be required today. Cautiously, I walked toward the door and knocked. There was a brief wait before it was opened, giving me time to build up a level of anxiety that I knew would be unhelpful. "Who are you?" I thought it best to scowl a little in the hope he would not think me a pushover. "David sent me." It was brief but told him all he needed to know. I was about to say, *"How are you today?"* but thought better of it. It was neither expected nor would it be appreciated. He looked at my head. I looked back at him, slightly puzzled, until I remembered he wanted the wig. I took it off and handed it over. He was in his late middle age and looked every bit a crook.

He led me through to a dingy office and I was invited to sit. This was difficult as I had the pistol in my pocket and by my reckoning, it was aimed at my crotch. The dilemma was not lost on him. "Are you looking to shoot me or your cock, boy?" He laughed. Foolishly, I stood and took the gun out of my pocket, and at that moment, one of his heavies grabbed me around the neck and I dropped it. I was unaware he was behind me. Cedric, meanwhile, began to unstitch the gems and what I assumed was cocaine from the wig, completely unperturbed. "Put him down, he's harmless. Are you new? I haven't seen you before, what's your name?" He continued to unpick the wig, putting the diamonds, which were the size of thumbnails, onto the desk. "Chris." I thought Christopher sounded too posh. "Well, Chris, what kind of earner are you on? Our David isn't the most generous of employers, where did he find you?" Even if Cedric decided not to pay me the full amount that I was due to collect, or chose to keep the stash, there would be little I could do. My pistol was firmly in his assistant's hand, the only consolation being that it was not pointing at a particular part of my anatomy that I might have use for later. He took his time examining the diamonds and weighed the powder. "10,000 rand, that's what we agreed, isn't it?" He was teasing - at least, I hoped he was. I thought I would play along with him. "I thought it was 100,000 rand?" He looked up at me and smiled. "He's funny this boy, I'll give him that."

He continued to study the gems. It occurred to me that I appeared to be adjusting far too well to my new job. This was a shady world where exploitation and greed were the cornerstones of success. People's lives were tossed about like pancakes on Shrove Tuesday. If they hit the ceiling or the floor, it mattered little or not at all, there was plenty more batter to use up. He handed me the wig and I ceremoniously put it on, adjusting the sides as I did. It was much lighter now. His assistant laughed. "Like wearing it, do ya'?" I saw his point. I had no use for the wig now the deal had been done. Cedric counted out the money and placed it down before me. "I'll count it if I may," I said poshly. "You will, my son. You will. I won't have David accuse me of short-changing him." I counted the money and agreed it was all there. He asked me to sign for the money, which I did. Without thinking, I then offered him my hand to shake. It was naive of me. I was not a salesman thanking a customer for his business. I was a drug and diamond mule delivering a consignment. They both laughed and he extended his arm and offered me his hand anyway. He gripped hard and I winced slightly. I was shown the door and given the pistol back, then I returned to the car with the money and wig as I had been instructed.

The driver took the money and the pistol but left me with the wig. "Keep that, you'll need it again. All the money there?" I was unsure now whether I should offer a cursory nod or engage in dialogue. I chose the latter. "Yes. It's all there, do you want to count it?" He smiled. "It had better be." With that, he started the car and we returned to the airport. He suggested I put the wig back on and kept it on until I got back to the hotel in Johannesburg. I followed the instruction.

By the time I got back to my bedroom, I was exhausted again. It was not so much the travel as the tension of not knowing what might happen. The temperature outside had also risen to 36 C. I wondered what Cedric had made of me and what he would do with the diamonds and the cocaine. Would he sell them in bulk or split them up and distribute through a network of dealers? Did it matter?

I decided not to nap. I'd shower and 'phone Caroline. I felt dirty, not in the physical sense, but needed to cleanse myself of the day. The shower was good. I lay on the bed and called Caroline. It rang for a few seconds before Caroline answered. "Is it okay for me to call?" There was a short pause before she responded. "Are you okay, what's happened?" She sounded genuinely worried for me. In that split second, I was unsure how to respond. I hadn't thought through what I would say before I 'phoned. Should I play down what I had experienced, or should I tell her the truth? I did not want to worry her but equally, I had to tell someone how I was feeling. If nothing else, I wanted to purge my soul, but I chose not to.

"I'm fine. Tired, but fine. How are you...where are you?" I thought I would turn the conversation around to her. "I'm so pleased to hear your voice. I haven't slept for worrying about you, worrying that you might be dead." Again, I wanted to distract her from my plight. "Where are you? Did you catch a flight back to London?" My ploy worked. "No. I stayed in Harare. I checked into a hotel. I am not sure I can return to London knowing you are out here. I tried to speak to David to persuade him to let you go although I did not want him to think I cared about you, but that I cared about being caught for abducting you. He showed no interest in what I had to say. He got angry with me and kept saying, *'That Bastard killed our sister, I'm not letting him off the hook'.* I would have been surprised if David had agreed to Caroline's request. Why would he? I was a commodity to be used and, likely, disposed of. I was not a human being in his eyes, but his sister's murderer. He lived a life of crime and murder was second nature to him. I tried to reassure Caroline that I was okay and avoided mentioning that I had killed Mr. Brammer, for I knew that just mentioning his name would release a well of remorse within me, and I would be incapable of continuing the conversation. There was a knock at the bedroom door. I put Caroline on hold and opened it. It was the bell boy, who handed me another envelope and a small parcel. I went back to Caroline and spent the next ten minutes talking idly before I hung up. I would call her again in a day or so.

I went down to the restaurant and had a hearty meal and far too much wine. The feeling of contentment reminded me of the supper I had had with Peter in the café and how *accommodating* Debbie had been. It seemed an age ago as the fond memories returned. I went back to my room. I had to read my latest orders.
There was a certain predictability to my instructions. *A driver would meet me in the lobby and take me to the airport*. This time, my destination was London. In the box I was to discover seven tubes of Alka Seltzer. They were all sealed. They had to contain diamonds; I was sure of it. There was also a 1 kg bag of Snowflake Cake wheat flour and by its touch, it seemed to be authentic. Clearly, this was cocaine, meth, or some other drug I had to traffic. I had no idea of its street value, but my guess was that it was substantial. For any smuggler, it was a sizeable consignment. I was to wear the wig, although it would serve no useful purpose other than to change my outward appearance. Security would be on the lookout for the supermarket gunman, a bearded man with thinning hair, not a clean-shaven man with a full head of hair. Of course, they may not even be on the lookout at all; after all, murder here was not uncommon.

I was instructed to put the tubes and the bag of flour into the briefcase, not in my suitcase. I was also issued with a new suit, shirt, and tie that I would wear for the journey. I was being portrayed as a legitimate businessman, not a smuggler of contraband. I was taking an international flight to London where security would be at his highest. As far as I could speculate, my chances of getting through undetected were slim. But then, would David risk losing so much booty, knowing there was a high probability I would be caught? He was not stupid, no matter how vindictive he was. Then again, he wanted the worst for me so I wondered if, rather than killing me himself, he might allow the penal system to do it for him. It was impossible to understand the mind of a psychopath. I knew I was unable to survive yet another lengthy prison sentence.

CHAPTER TWENTY-FIVE -

LONDON

Morning arrived. The air conditioning had done its duty. Aside from the odd hour or two of being wide awake, wondering how and when this would all end, I slept well. I went down to breakfast; after all, it might be my last for a long time. The desk clerk acknowledged me. He knew the beardless man with the full head of hair. I smiled. The restaurant was busy. I was shown a table and helped myself to the buffet. My driver was sitting at the other side of the restaurant but did not see me. I thought it best if we kept our distance. I ate breakfast and read a well-thumbed newspaper that was light on news but heavy on advertising. As I got up to leave, my driver had gone. I returned to my room before leaving for the airport.

I was apprehensive as we drew up outside the terminal building. There was no chit chat. I grabbed the briefcase and suitcase from the trunk and went inside. I checked in and went for a coffee. I thought I would make the most of my freedom before joining the queue for security. A table had become vacant. As I sat down, a businesswoman asked to join me. She was also travelling to London for a medical conference. It was her first trip to England, and she was excited at the prospect. My accent led her to believe I was Australian, not British, which I thought odd. My mind was firmly focused on what I would do if I were stopped at security, so I found it hard to fully answer the barrage of questions she was aiming at me. My coffee gradually went cold. Eventually, I wished her well and slowly made my way to passport control. I was becoming self-conscious. My wig had slipped on one side and I wondered what the officer would make of me as I handed over my passport. He simply looked up and wished me a good flight. It was too late to go to the men's room. I would have to navigate security before I did, and the last thing I wanted was to draw attention to myself. I joined a queue and put my briefcase down, and as I rose, I tugged at the wig in the hope that my adjustment had worked. I would have to wait to find out. I reached the carousel and put my personal belongings and the briefcase in the bin provided, then watched it sail into the x-ray machine. I walked through the security arch and waited for the briefcase to come out the other side. I was sweating, the palms of my hands and forehead were wet. I was not cut out for this type of work. I kept my eyes on the operative sat behind the screen monitoring the bags as they went through. She was distracted by a colleague and looked away as the briefcase meandered its way toward me. I picked up the bag and walked away. To say my heart was racing would be an understatement. I headed straight for the nearest men's room. Sweat was seeping from every orifice and my head was itching like mad. My adjustment had worked the wig was stable and sat correctly on my head, but I had to take it off to relieve myself of the irritation. Two other people were at the mirror. I was unperturbed what they thought as I removed it.

I decided to reward myself with a bottle of water and a newspaper, knowing it would be a long flight. I boarded the flight within the hour. Again, it was full to bursting. I had a window seat and slept for most of the journey. As we began to descend into Heathrow airport, I knew my biggest challenge would be getting through customs and security. My track record of staying calm was mixed. I thought I handled the meeting with Cedric quite well. I was calm and almost collected and had avoided sweating too much. The same could not be said for my encounter with Mr. Brammer. I wondered how that traumatic event was still being played out in the minds of his family and colleagues. It was tragic. My test earlier at Jan Smuts security had affected me in a way I could not allow to reoccur at Heathrow. Sweating is a key sign that security look for in passengers and I knew I had to hide it and the only way was to relax. I tried to put the subject out of my mind and turned to the passenger next to me. He was just waking, and I wished him a good morning. We spoke for ten minutes until we touched down, he was a sales manager for a south African flour miller. Their brand was 'Snowflake', which was precisely what I had in my briefcase. How bizarre, I thought. I chose not to mention that I was a brand devotee and happened to be carrying a 1 kg bag in my briefcase. He had likely never imagined that his company was being used as a front for drug smuggling. Small world.

We landed and I gradually worked my way to the front of the plane to disembark. As I shuffled forward, I gave myself a stiff talking to. I had to stay relaxed, confident, and positive of mind. I was a businessman returning to the UK after seeing customers in Johannesburg. I would think on my feet – I had no option. There was a long line at passport control. Gradually I approached the barrier, passport in one hand, briefcase in the other. I checked my forehead and was relieved to find that sweat had not reached my head, although my shirt was sopping wet. I tried not to fidget or remind myself that my head was itching again, I could do absolutely nothing about it. Trying to focus one's mind on something, anything other than the thing it wants to concentrate on, is not easy. I should have taken up yoga. It was my turn. I greeted the officer with a smile and asked how he was. He smiled and looked me in the eyes. "No beard anymore?" My passport photo had me with my previous facial hair and what was on my head was far less voluptuous. He was used to spotting anything out of the ordinary and there was so much different from the photo with the person standing before him. My mind flashed back to my trial when I heard the judge pass sentence. I remembered being taken down and wondered if this were just the start of another long, drawn out saga that would see me back inside. "No, my children begged me to shave it off for charity." He smiled and responded "I've been there before. My penance was a charity run. I had never run in my life. They found it quite amusing." I was so relieved that my lie had resonated with him, distracting him from the truth. He stamped my passport. I smiled and walked through the barrier. I had a broad grin on my face but at least it was better than a grimace. The boy done good. I could not relax, though: far from it. I had yet to pass through Customs. On the many occasions I had returned to Heathrow on an international flight I had just breezed through often without an officer in sight. But every time I had, despite knowing I had nothing to declare, I had still felt guilty. I was searched on one occasion but knowing they would find nothing of any interest it was easy. I hoped I would breeze through today. I waited at the carousel for my suitcase and it was one of the first to arrive. I scooped it up and started the walk of trepidation to Customs. I continued to sweat profusely but my face remained dry, which was the main thing. I hummed a tune in my head to distract me from the mental anguish I was really suffering. Every stride I took felt as though my shoes were caked in mud, as they had been with Peter when we tried to find the allotment. My legs were like lead. I tried not to move my eyes too much avoiding the look of a rabbit in the headlights. I was twenty or so paces in when a customs officer appeared from nowhere and asked to see my bags.

"Good morning, sir, where have you travelled from? Mind if I see your bags?" "Johannesburg. No, please go ahead." What I wanted to say was, *"No, I'd be grateful if you didn't. I have contraband I don't want you to find"*. "Business or pleasure"? Idle chat was a part of the job, designed to test a person's confidence - or lack thereof. I had to think on my feet. "Oh, business. Flour. I'm looking to import flour from Africa." *Well, that was original*, I thought to myself. Of course, my subconscious was also saying to me, *"There is a bag of flour in your briefcase... what an odd thing to be carrying!"* If you can *establish a reason for having it before he finds it, it might go your way!* "Flour. So, in the business, are you?" At this point, he was rummaging through my suitcase, but he would find nothing there. He meticulously went through all the items of clothing and my bathroom bag containing items I had taken from the hotel bathroom, including a nail file, a mending kit, shower hat, shampoo and conditioner, and a shoehorn! Next, having removed all the items from the case, he set about examining the case itself. He ran his hands along the side panel and the lid and carcass of the case but found nothing. "I have a friend who's a buyer at a major supermarket and he's on the lookout for new brands to sell, so I thought there might be an opportunity to research the market and come up with some options." *Really? Did that sound at all plausible?* "Odd thing to be interested in. I thought we produced enough flour in this country?" Thinking on my feet was proving ever more difficult. My head was demanding I took the bloody wig off and scratched until late afternoon. I could feel my body temperature reach boiling point and my crotch was sweating so much that I glanced down to see whether a wet stain had appeared on my trousers. I was beginning to lose it, but I had to persist. "Yes, we produce a lot of grain in the UK and our milling business is one of the most economically productive in the world. Of course, we are a small country, relatively speaking, but the supermarkets are always looking to offer customers something different. I found a brand out there I think will do the trick, though. It's called *Snowflake Cake wheat flour."* Not only had I introduced into the conversation that I was 'in flour', but I had also named the brand that he would find in the briefcase. But would it work? "Interesting stuff. Which supermarket?" "Oh, Sainsbury's", I squeaked. "And your friend's name - who's the buyer?" It came so easily. "Caroline De Jong." I thought my response was swift enough to end the conversation there, but not a bit. "Is she English? Sounds like a foreign name?" I felt like saying, *"Foreigners do live and work in the UK you know, or hadn't you noticed?"* It seemed an unwise statement to make. I wanted him to be my best friend and I also wanted him to think that I was serious about the opportunity flour had presented me with, especially *Snowflake Wheat flour.* "She's Zimbabwean. Her family were farmers before Mugabe turned them out." Again, it was a smart thing to say, I thought. He would likely be a patriot and would have been appalled by Mugabe's antics at the time, repatriating white farmers' land to the indigenous population. Then again, I had no way of knowing. He offered no response and turned his attention to the briefcase.

He pressed the button and the clasp flicked open. He looked inside and took out the mobile 'phone Caroline had given me, a newspaper from the day before that I had omitted to throw away, a magazine I had picked up at the hotel, seven tubes of Alka Selzer, and a bag of Snowflake wheat flour. "So, this is the flour you mentioned?" Of course, it was, what else? "Yes, that's it. A small bag. A sample." "Do you get indigestion?" I was thrown by the question. "Indigestion?" Of course, he was referring to the Alka Selzer tubes. "Yes, all the time." Having a pack of something to relieve indigestion was one thing, but seven tubes? Really? That is precisely what came next. "Seven tubes? Seems a lot to be carrying." I was panicking now. *Where do I go from here*, I thought? I chose to say nothing. He left the tubes and flour on the table and said he would be back shortly. He disappeared behind the two-way glass screens, no doubt to check them out and discuss with colleagues. I stood there, believing all eyes were on me and every move I made. Every facial expression, yawn, scratching of the nose, or flickering of the eyes was probably being observed for signs of guilt. The itch caused by wearing the wig became so intense that I simply had to try and scratch my head without drawing too much attention or accidentally pulling the wretched thing off. I gained some sense of relief knowing that the wig was diamond and cocaine free.

Ten minutes past and I stood there aimlessly, awaiting my fate. Eventually, he returned with another officer. "We'd like to take a sample of the flour and open one of the tubes. Is that okay with you?" Of course, it was not okay with me, but I had no choice in the matter. I watched them as they snipped the outer bag containing the so-called flour and took a sample. They broke the seal on one of the tubes and opened it. My eyes were wide open, and the sweat was pouring from every gland in my body. My face was dripping. It was over. I had to accept I would be led away and the rest of my life with Caroline would be extinguished, just as the flame had done from the lamp in the allotment shed with Peter those years ago. "Are you okay, sir?" He looked at me and noticed I was in trouble. "Yes, it's been a long trip and I'm dehydrated." His colleague fetched a glass of water which I gulped down as though it would be my last. He offered me a seat, which I gratefully accepted. He continued to open the tube until the lid was fully off. He tipped it to the side and a tablet dropped into his hand. Then, he removed the rest of the contents. It was full of tablets. Once again, he went behind the glass screen, presumably to conduct a Nic test to determine whether they were drugs. The end was nigh. When he returned, his colleague left him to it and went back behind the screen. "Thank you, sir. Thanks for your patience. Will you be okay? You can pack your bags now."

Pack my bags? I was dumbfounded to say the least. I repacked my suitcase and told him that I was okay. I was more than okay - I was ecstatic. Why hadn't they detected drugs in the tablets and the flour? Clearly, I was not carrying contraband. So, why was I carrying them? It dawned on me. This was a part of David's plan to put me through as much pain and anguish as possible. He would have me suffer right up to the point at which he or one of his cronies would kill me.

I walked through to the concourse and immediately 'phoned Caroline back in Harare before the driver located me. She answered immediately. She was in a flap and asked me not to say anything until I heard what she had to say. Soon after I had last spoken to her, David had called her, demanding they both return immediately to the UK, to meet me at Heathrow. They had got a flight which arrived some hours earlier and had been met by David's driver. They would take me a short distance away from the airport, where he intended to shoot me. She had to go along with the plan. She was in the Ladies room on the concourse, not far from where I was. David was waiting for me. Then, she ended the call. I looked around and saw David. I made out I had not seen him, but by the time I had cleared the barrier and was walking toward the exit, he'd caught up with me and grabbed my arm. Caroline appeared behind him. "Just follow me to the car." The three of us left the terminal building and a driver was waiting for us in the obligatory black Mercedes. I got into the front seat, the driver got out and handed something to David and Caroline. David and Caroline got into the back. We drove off. "I wasn't expecting to see you two", I blurted out. There was no response. No more than five minutes later, we entered a large car park which was full. David and Caroline got out and my driver held his hand out as if to say *wait here.* I could hear them arguing, although it was impossible to comprehend what they were saying. David approached my door and dragged me out. His driver got out too and came round to us. I looked squarely into David's eyes and saw that same evil look I had witnessed when I first encountered him in Harare before he punched and kicked me to the ground. I felt sure this look was not one he reserved for me alone. No, it was a necessary part of his profession. He needed to look angry and in control. Importantly, to gain and maintain respect, he had to have all the qualities of the psychopath, which included being prepared to say or do anything to get his way. Of course, that included murder without a conscience.

Surprisingly, though, I had a sense of my own confidence. I had been through an ordeal these past few days and it had toughened me up. I had met some seriously undesirable people and I had murdered a man, Mr. Brammer, in cold blood at David's behest. Now, I was a killer myself. Unlike David and his subordinates, though, I was not a psychopath. I still had a conscience. That shooting would haunt me for the rest of my life. David punched me in the stomach and as I rolled forward, I felt the full force of his knee in my face. Blood oozed from my nose and I nearly passed out. He picked me up, forced me against the car, and put his face close to mine. I had full vision of those callous eyes, which revealed a soulless man who had no compunction about killing on a whim. He was well-educated and had had everything going for him in life, but he had chosen a life of crime. He did not find crime, crime found him. Psychopaths seek power and influence and what better and more lucrative way is there to gain sustenance than wielding that power over people who have moral standards, who put others before themselves, who put society before personal greed, and loving relationships before killing people? I felt truly, sorry for him. He yelled at me as he had in Harare, but again, I failed to hear him. What he said, what he thought of me, his belief that I had killed his sister – none of it mattered a jot. I knew I was innocent but there was no chance of convincing him, even if I tried my hardest as I had done before. There was nothing he could do now that would have me cowering or begging for my life. I deserved to die. I had killed a man in cold blood. An eye for an eye.

In the background, drowned out by David's verbal attack on me, I heard Caroline. She was begging him to let me go. The more she screamed and tugged at his arm, the more manic he became. His driver grabbed me and held my arms as David punched me again and again. This had to be the end game. I would die here, ingloriously, in a London car park and be abandoned for a stranger to find.

It is a strange phenomenon: when the mind and body is subjected to such an assault, it switches off. There is no pain, only thoughts, and imaginings. I was reliving my guilt in ending Mr. Brammer's life. I was thinking of Eleanor, Peter, the bookshop, the tunnel, and my time in Winchester. I caught the smell in my nostrils of a shrub I often passed on my way back to the cottage after visiting the OV. It was as though I had already passed to the other side and my life had ended as the blows continued to rain down upon me.

I was woken out of my trace by a single, sudden gunshot. Confused, I wondered if I was hearing the pistol Peter had used to kill Mary's husband after leaving the train on that fateful day. I noticed that David had stopped beating me. His head and torso had gone limp and he fell to the ground. Then, I heard a second shot. This time, David's driver released me from his grip as blood spurted from his head and gushed all over me. He, too, fell unceremoniously to the ground. Too weak to stand, I fell forward on top of David. As I looked skyward, I saw her. It was Caroline, arm outstretched, pistol in hand. She had shot them both.

I remember little of what happened next. Caroline dragged me to the Mercedes and laid me on the back seat. I was barely conscious. She programmed the sat nav for the cottage in Winchester. Everything else was a blur. The first thing I recall was Caroline bathing my face. She had managed to get me into the cottage, unaided, and I had been there recuperating for two days.

As I recovered with Caroline as my devoted nurse, I thought of David and his driver lying dead in the car park. Some would argue that it was a fitting end for psychopaths. The world would be better off without them. I found that a difficult concept to embrace. There is good in all of us, and for all their sins and failings - and there were many - David was a human being. He was wired differently from most, but was that of his own making?

We all live a life. For some, it can be wholesome and fulfilling, working to earn a living to raise a family and supporting community. In many respects, it can be a predictable life and there is nothing wrong with that. In fact, if I could turn back the clock, that is probably the life I would have chosen for myself. The philosopher in me says *that none of us choose the life we lead. Instead, we experience the life for which we are destined.* David was destined for a dramatic end to his life and he probably knew that would be the case, but did he care? It went with the territory. What he could not have imagined in his wildest nightmare was that Caroline would be his executioner, his only remaining sister. Eleanor's death was a tragedy, and to this day, I cannot reconcile in my head who killed her and why. Was it a suicide? I will never know. Peter's life, too, had been tragically cut short. I believed he was a good man, despite his inability to control his emotions. Shooting Mary's husband had changed everything. Unlike David, though, he had no way of channeling his emotions. The psychopath in David believed that he would always be on top by harnessing the traits that Peter possessed.

I stared aimlessly out of the window. It started to rain quite hard, the kind of rain that hits the pavement at high speed and bounces back at you. People rushed by the window, absorbed in their own cocooned world. It was then that I saw her. She was stunningly attractive and elegantly dressed in a long, jet-black coat, with a rust brown fur collar that fitted tightly around her neck. She held high a bright red umbrella that matched her lipstick. She stood motionless, ignoring the torrential rain that enveloped her and the people that scampered past. The sadness in her face told a story. Her arms were crossed as though she were standing at the graveside of a loved one, bidding a final farewell.

Caroline was beautiful and I was in love with her.

Understandably, she never got over shooting dead her brother and his driver. The memories haunted her in the months and years that followed, as did my murder of Mr. Brammer. Eleanor's memory never faded in my mind nor did her mystery death. I still think of Peter and often read his letter. Such a wasted life.

We lived the rest of our lives together in the cottage, knowing what others did not. We were killers both, but I like to think righteous killers. We could never be exonerated for our crimes nor should we be. We would carry the burden of guilt to our graves.

Printed in Poland
by Amazon Fulfillment
Poland Sp. z o.o., Wrocław
02 March 2023

7a3946c1-878d-45ad-b5bc-04da159eccaaR01